ICE

LOLLY

PETERBOROUGH PUBLIC LIBRARY   JUN - - 2010

Also by Jean Ure

Love and Kisses
Fortune Cookie
Star Crazy Me!
Over the Moon
Boys Beware
Sugar and Spice
Is Anybody There?
Secret Meeting
Passion Flower
Shrinking Violet
Boys on the Brain
Skinny Melon and Me
Becky Bananas, This is Your Life!
Fruit and Nutcase
The Secret Life of Sally Tomato
Family Fan Club

Special three-in-one editions

The Tutti-Frutti Collection
The Flower Power Collection
The Friends Forever Collection

And for younger readers

Dazzling Danny
Daisy May
Monster in the Mirror

ICE LOLLY

Jean Ure

HarperCollins *Children's Books*

PETERBOROUGH PUBLIC LIBRARY

For Tamesha Pria

First published in Great Britain by HarperCollins *Children's Books* in 2010
HarperCollins *Children's Books* is a division of HarperCollins*Publishers* Ltd,
77-85 Fulham Palace Road, Hammersmith, London W6 8JB

The HarperCollins *Children's Books* website address is
www.harpercollins.co.uk

1

Ice Lolly
Text © Jean Ure 2010
Illustrations © HarperCollins*Publishers* 2010

The author and illustrator assert the moral right to be
identified as the author and illustrator of this work.

ISBN-13: 978-0-00-728173-2

Printed and bound in England by
Clays Ltd, St Ives plc

Conditions of Sale
This book is sold subject to the condition that it shall not,
by way of trade or otherwise, be lent, re-sold, hired out or otherwise
circulated without the publisher's prior consent in any form, binding or
cover other than that in which it is published and without a similar condition
including this condition being imposed on the subsequent purchaser.

Mixed Sources
Product group from well-managed
forests and other controlled sources
FSC   www.fsc.org Cert no. SW-COC-1806
© 1996 Forest Stewardship Council

FSC is a non-profit international organisation established to promote the
responsible management of the world's forests. Products carrying the FSC
label are independently certified to assure consumers that they come
from forests that are managed to meet the social, economic and
ecological needs of present and future generations.

Find out more about HarperCollins and the environment at
www.harpercollins.co.uk/green

CHAPTER ONE

So this is it; it's happening. I'm sitting here between Auntie Ellen and Uncle Mark in this room that's called a chapel, though it isn't my idea of what a chapel ought to be. Chapels should be beautiful, I think; this is just plain and ordinary. Maybe that is what you get for not believing in God. But you can't be a hypocrite, just for the sake of a stained-glass window. You can't say you believe when you don't. Not however much you would like to. Mum wouldn't have wanted me to do that. She used to say, "You have to face up to things, Lol." So that is what I am doing. I am facing up.

We are sitting in the front row, which is reserved for family. But anyone else could have sat here if they'd wanted; I wouldn't have minded. There's lots of room, only a few people have come. There's Stevie, of course. Why isn't she sitting with us? She is practically family. Far more than Auntie Ellen or Uncle Mark, even if Uncle Mark *is* Mum's brother. Mum used to say that Stevie was a rock. Even Uncle Mark agrees that we couldn't have managed without her. Auntie Ellen just curls her lip and calls her "that dreadful old woman from next door". She says she looks like a bag lady, meaning someone who lives on the street and carries all her worldly possessions in a plastic bin bag. I think that is such a horrid thing to say.

I know that Stevie dresses kind of weirdly and smells of cat, but I can think of worse things to smell of, and what does it matter how people dress? Today she is wearing her best coat that she got from a charity shop. It is dark purple and reaches to the ground, so that all you can see of her big clumpy boots are the tips, poking out from underneath. Originally the coat had fur round the collar, but Stevie doesn't approve of fur so she ripped it off and gave it to the cats to play with. Unfortunately, most of the collar came off with it, so I have to admit she does look a bit peculiar, especially as she has put on her see-through plastic rain hat. She told me that she was going to wear her rain hat, specially. She said, "You have to be dressed properly, for church. I wouldn't want to let you down."

Generally speaking, Stevie doesn't give a rap. It's one of her expressions. She is always shouting it out. "Don't give a rap!" So I am really touched that she has gone to so much trouble. I think that Mum would be touched too, and agree that Stevie ought to wear her rain hat even though this is only a chapel, and a very plain and boring chapel, and nothing to do with church. And *I* don't give a rap if she looks like a bag lady and makes people stare. She was Mum's friend and Mum loved her.

Apart from Stevie, the only other people are Temeeka's mum from over the road, and Mr and Mrs Miah from the corner shop, plus some of the people from Mum's office where she used to work before she got sick. I don't really know the people from her office, as I was only eight when Mum had to stop working. But they all came and spoke to me while we were waiting to come in, and two of the women kissed me. One of the men is standing up and talking. He's talking about Mum. I am trying not to listen. I know he's saying nice things, because that's what people do, but I *am not going to listen*. I am squeezing my eyes tight shut and concentrating very hard… I am building a wall, brick by brick, like a fortress. Soon it will be finished and then nothing will be able to reach me. But for the moment there is still this chink, this tiny chink, where things might be able to slip through. I have to keep them out!

Auntie Ellen wasn't sure that I should be here today.

She said why didn't I stay at Stevie's until it was over.

"Then we'll come and fetch you, and take you home."

She thought that it would be too much for me. She probably thought that I would cry. Well, I haven't! I haven't even sniffled. I am frozen, behind my brick wall. Like in an ice house, where in olden days, before they invented refrigerators, they used to store blocks of ice, hidden underground, deep and dark, where the sun could not get at them. *The ice never melted.* So she doesn't have to keep shooting those anxious glances at me. Mum never cried, and I am not going to, either.

They haven't brought Holly and Michael with them, and I am glad about that. They have always disapproved of Mum and me. Well, Holly has. So have Auntie Ellen and Uncle Mark, of course, but they are grown-ups. You have to accept it from grown-ups. But I don't like being disapproved of by someone that is two years my junior. She is only ten years old! What right does she have to be disapproving?

I stop thinking about Holly and Michael and stare

fixedly ahead at what looks like a spider crawling up the wall. Do you get spiders in chapels? I suppose you get them pretty well everywhere. But what would a spider find to live on? It is so cold in here, and bare.

Maybe it isn't a spider. I wriggle a bit, and Auntie Ellen shoots me one of her glances. The man from Mum's office is still talking, he is saying something about Mum having a wicked sense of humour.

"She used to keep us all in stitches! I remember, one time…"

I scuttle back inside my ice house. I am safe in here. I think of Mr Pooter in his cardboard carrying-box in the car. How long will it be before I can go to him? He will be so confused, he is not used to being shut away. I wish he could have come in with us! I know it's what Mum would have wanted. After me and Stevie, Mr Pooter was the person she loved best in all the world. Maybe she even loved him more than she loved Stevie. But they would have been bound to say no if I'd suggested bringing him. Auntie Ellen has already hinted that it would be far better if I gave him to Stevie.

"She's a cat woman."

The way she said it, it was like a kind of sneering. Like Stevie is old and dotty and mad. Just because she loves cats! She has devoted her life to them. She has eleven at the moment, all of them rescued. Auntie Ellen, with one of her sniffs that she does, said that "one more wouldn't make much difference. You can hardly move for cats as it is". I feel good that I stood up to her. Mum would have approved! *She* wouldn't want me and Mr Pooter to be parted from each other. But I know Auntie Ellen only gave way in the end because Uncle Mark told her to. I know she's not pleased. She really doesn't care about animals.

The man from Mum's office has finished talking and is returning to his seat. I wonder about what is going to happen next. I have never been to anything like this before.

I have never been to a funeral before.

There. I have said it. But it's all right, I am safe in my ice house. I am frozen, I feel nothing.

I am thinking back to when my gran died. I was only three, so I don't really remember very much, except that Mum was sad and that we lived in a flat somewhere near Oxford and that Dad was still with us. And then later on Mum got sad all over again, only this time she was sad because Dad had started shouting a lot and growing angry. So next thing I remember is Dad going off and not coming back and me and Mum being on our own and moving to London and living next door to Stevie. I was six years old by then. I had to start at a new school, which frightened me, as I had only just got used to my other one. Mum said she was so, so sorry, but begged me to be brave. She said that life was full of changes.

"It's a bit like books, all divided up into different chapters."

She said that if Oxford had been Chapter 1, then London was Chapter 2. And then she hugged me and said, "Oh, but Lol, there will be so many more to come!" Like she thought that was a good thing. But I never wanted any more; I just wanted Chapter 2 to go on for ever. Only nothing ever does. You don't realise that when you're just six years old.

Mrs Miah has been standing up and talking about Mum. I feel guilty that I haven't been listening, but maybe she would understand. Now she has gone back to her seat, and I think perhaps things are almost over. Nobody else has got up to speak, and somewhere off stage they are playing Mum's song that I chose.

Though the final curtain's fallen
And we two have had to part
My love still marches onward
To the drumbeat of my heart.

I can feel Auntie Ellen exchanging glances over my head with Uncle Mark. They don't approve. Auntie Ellen doesn't think the song is appropriate. She tried really hard to get me to change my mind.

"I'm not saying it has to be a hymn, necessarily, but at least something a bit more – well! Classical, maybe. Isn't there anything classical that your mum liked?"

Mum liked all sorts of music, but this was the song that she would have wanted. It was one of her big favourites. She used to say it was her inheritance track that she'd inherited from *her* mum.

"Your gran used to play it all the time after she lost your grandad."

I know that this is a really sad song, but it was special to Mum, and that makes it special to me. In any case, it was up to me to choose, not Auntie Ellen.

Now everybody is standing up. Uncle Mark stands up, so I do too.

"All right?" He looks down at me, and I nod. We file out, into the cold sunshine. I hold my head very high.

The women from Mum's office kiss me again before going off to their car. The man who did the talking tells me that it was "a privilege to have known your mother. She was a very special lady". I look at him stony-faced. Uncle Mark puts his arm round my shoulders and in slightly reproving tones says, "That is something we must always remember." He thinks I am being ungracious. He doesn't realise I am in my ice house, frozen like a fish finger.

Stevie comes over. She says, "Well, then!" She won't kiss me; she never does. I suppose, really, she is quite a gruff kind of person. But I am glad. I don't want to be kissed or made a fuss of.

Stevie scratches her head, under her plastic rain hat. She has probably got a flea from one of her cats.

"I'll be going now," she says.

She turns and stomps off, down the path. Uncle Mark calls after her. "Are you sure you don't want a lift?" But Stevie just waves a hand and goes clumping on. Uncle Mark shakes his head. He says it's a long walk for an old woman. "It must be a good mile."

I tell him that Stevie walks everywhere. "She doesn't approve of cars."

"Tough as old boots," says Auntie Ellen. She's sneering again. I don't think she has any right to sneer, after all that Stevie did for me and Mum.

I say goodbye to Temeeka's mum, who kisses me and says, "Chin up, luvvie!" I say goodbye to Mr and Mrs Miah. Mrs Miah also kisses me, but Mr Miah takes my hand.

"We shall miss you," he says.

Auntie Ellen is growing impatient. She wants us to get a move on. She says we have a long journey ahead of us and the traffic will be horrendous at this time of day.

I hurry after her to the car. I can see that Mr Miah has something more he would like to say, and I don't want to seem rude, but I am worried about Mr Pooter. I cram myself into the back seat and pull his carrying box on to my lap. It is an old cardboard one of Stevie's, a bit crushed and battered. I waggle my finger through one of the air holes and hear a chirrup. I relax. If he's chirruping, it means he's happy.

There's not much room on the back seat as it is piled with boxes. The whole car is crowded out with boxes. We got them from Mr Miah, and me and Stevie spent all yesterday filling them. Auntie Ellen had already warned me that there wouldn't be room for everything.

"We don't have much cupboard space, so try to be a bit selective. Just bring what's most important. Clothes, obviously."

But clothes are the *least* important. What's most important, apart from Mr Pooter, is books. Mum loved her books! I have packed all of them. Every single one. I told Stevie she could have everything that was left over for the local Animal Samaritans. I know that's what Mum would have wanted.

Auntie Ellen turned a bit pale when she saw how many boxes there were. She said, "Laurel, I told you to be selective!"

I said that I had been. "Most of it's books."

"*Books?*" She almost shrieked it. I wanted to giggle, cos it was like I'd said I'd packed up a load of tarantulas, or something. Imagine being scared of books! She looked across at Uncle Mark and said, "Now what do we do? We don't have room for all this lot!"

Uncle Mark said that we didn't have time to start unpacking. "We'll just have to sort it out the other end."

Auntie Ellen wanted me to leave some of the boxes behind, but I wouldn't. So here they all are, and here are me and Mr Pooter, squashed up against them. I wish we could have gone to live with Stevie. I'm sure she wouldn't have minded Mum's books, not even if they did have to be kept in heaps on the floor. Stevie isn't houseproud like Auntie Ellen. But of course they wouldn't let me. They said it wasn't a *suitable placement*, meaning there are cats roaming everywhere and it isn't hygienic. People are a great deal too bothered about hygiene, if you ask me. Stevie seems to have lived quite happily all these years without being troubled by it. They'd probably have said me and Mum weren't hygienic, either. We didn't go in very much for housework. We had more important things to worry about than dust, or cobwebs, or whether there was a rim round the bath – which I now realise there was, since Auntie Ellen remarked on it only this morning, shuddering as she did so. People care about the weirdest things.

I stare out of the window, wondering where we are.

Auntie Ellen says, "I told you the traffic would be bad." Uncle Mark says it's no problem. Once we hit the motorway we'll be all right.

"Assuming there aren't any hold-ups," says Auntie Ellen.

I think to myself that Auntie Ellen is one of those people who enjoy looking on the black side. Uncle Mark catches my eye in the driving mirror.

"OK back there?"

I nod, without speaking, and bury my nose in Mr Pooter's fur. I've opened his box so that we can have a cuddle.

"Home in time for tea," says Uncle Mark.

I force my lips into a smile. He is trying so hard to make me feel wanted, though I am sure I can't really be. I know Auntie Ellen doesn't want me. And I don't suppose Holly does, either. They are only taking me because they feel it's their duty. I know I ought to be grateful, and I am doing my best, but it is not easy. I would so much rather have gone to live with Stevie!

Mr Pooter sits up and rubs his head against mine. I rub back. Auntie Ellen says, "You make sure that cat doesn't start jumping about."

I tell her that Mr Pooter is too old to jump about. Mum had him before she was married. "He's almost sixteen."

Auntie Ellen says she doesn't care. "It's not safe, having a cat loose in the car."

I close up one side of the box, so that it looks like he's shut away. I keep my hand in there, to reassure him. Mr Pooter purrs and dribbles.

"Motorway coming up," says Uncle Mark. "Home before you know it!"

Up until last week, home was the cottage that I shared with Mum. Old, and crumbly, and tiny as a dolls' house, with a narrow strip of garden going down to the railway. Now I shall be living on an estate, with hundreds of houses all the same, and everything bright and new. Our cottage was cosy, even if we did have a rim round the bath and cobwebs hanging from the ceiling. Uncle Mark's house is not cosy. It is too tidy. And too *clean*.

Uncle Mark looks at me again, in the mirror. "It's been a while," he says, "hasn't it?"

I don't understand what he means.

"Since you were last with us," he says.

I say, "Oh." And then, "Yes."

"You must have been about Holly's age. The age she is now."

The Christmas before last. I was ten and a half. I'm thinking back. Remembering me and Mum, wrapping up presents at the last minute, waiting for Uncle Mark to come and fetch us. I can hear Mum saying that we must be on our best behaviour and not do anything to upset Auntie Ellen.

"It's very good of her to put up with us."

I remember being cheeky and telling Mum that she was the one that did all the upsetting. "Arguing about politics and stuff." And Mum saying that this year she wasn't going to even mention politics. "And if anyone else does, I shall just keep quiet."

To which I said, "*Ha ha.*" But Mum insisted that she meant it. She said it was very bad manners, in someone else's house. "Though I suppose," she added, "we shall have to watch the Queen's speech." And then she snatched up a cereal bowl and balanced it on her head, like a crown, and posed, all regal, on her chair. "*My husband and I...*"

Mum was brilliant at being the Queen. She sounded just like her! I give a sudden squawk of laughter. Auntie Ellen springs round.

"What's the matter?"

Nothing's the matter. I'm just remembering Mum, being the Queen. I stick my head inside Mr Pooter's box, to stifle another squawk which is about to burst out of me.

"What's so funny?" says Uncle Mark.

I can't tell him; he would think I was being rude. Mum said afterwards that our behaviour was unforgivable. But it was her fault! We were all sitting there on Christmas Day, in front of the television, waiting for the Queen to get going, when Mum leant across and whispered in my ear, *"My husband and I..."* and I immediately started giggling and couldn't stop. So then Mum started giggling and *she* couldn't stop. We just sat there, helpless, with Auntie Ellen growing more and more offended, which I suppose you can't really blame her for, what with it being her house, and us being her guests.

I can't remember whether we were invited last Christmas or not. Mum was in her wheelchair by then. Everything was getting a bit difficult for her, so we probably couldn't have gone anyway. But most likely we weren't invited, cos of having disgraced ourselves.

"Lol?" We've come off the motorway and pulled up at some traffic lights. Uncle Mark turns to look at me. "You sure you're OK?"

I tell him yes. I try to force my lips back into a smile, but this time they won't do it. I know Uncle Mark is only trying to be kind, but he shouldn't call me Lol! That was one of Mum's names for me. Lol, Lolly. Lollipop. Lol was for every day. Lollipop was when I was little. Lolly was for fun. I suppose now that I am frozen, I am an ice lolly…

That is a good joke! *Ice Lolly*. I wish I could tell Mum, we would have had such a laugh about it together. We laughed at most things, me and Mum. We didn't believe in being miserable.

Mr Pooter reaches out a paw and dabs at my face.

"Laurel, I told you before, *put that cat back in its box!*" thunders Auntie Ellen.

The Ice Lolly does what she is told. She closes the box and sits, frozen, staring straight ahead.

"That's better," says Auntie Ellen.

CHAPTER TWO

I'm upstairs in my bedroom. My *new* bedroom, in my new home. I've been here four days, now. I suppose I'll get used to it in time, though it is a bit like living in a foreign country where everyone has different customs and speaks a different language. However hard I try, I know that I don't really fit in. Auntie Ellen blames Mum;

I heard her say so to Uncle Mark. She said, "What can you expect, with that upbringing?"

When she says things like that, it makes me think that I just won't bother, I'll just go on being me. Except that if you are in someone else's house, that is maybe not very polite. Mum always insisted on good manners. It is why she was so cross with us for giggling during the Queen's speech. I wish she was here! I wish I could ask her what to do.

Holly is standing in the doorway, watching. "You going to get started?" she says.

I'm supposed to be choosing books to go on the bookshelf that Uncle Mark has put up for me. I've opened all the boxes, and very slowly, one by one, I'm taking out the books.

"Better get a move on," says Holly. "Be here all day, otherwise."

I know that she's right. But there are far more books than there's room for on the bookshelf. The shelf will only take about thirty. All the rest are going to have to be put back in their boxes and shut away in the loft. How can I possibly decide which ones get to stay and which ones are banished?

"Just pick your favourites," says Holly. She makes it sound easy. But it's not! They are all my favourites. Well, Mum's favourites. I hate the thought of Mum's books being sent into exile. I say this to Holly, and she looks at me like I'm something from another planet.

"They're only *books*," she says. This is what I mean about people speaking a different language. "Keep the ones with the nicest covers."

I tell her that you don't choose a book by its cover, but Holly says that way they'll look good on the shelf. "Specially if you get them all the same size, so they line up. It's untidy when some are short and some are tall. I think you should just have paperbacks, then you'll get more in." I guess she's trying to be helpful. She's come into the room and is rummaging about in the boxes, in search of books with nice covers that are all the same size. She takes one out and pulls a face. "What's this, all falling to pieces?"

It's *Middlemarch*. I have to admit it hasn't got a very nice cover, and it is a bit tatty. Me and Mum found it in an Oxfam shop.

"Don't want to keep that," says Holly. She tosses *Middlemarch* on to the bed. Mr Pooter, who is snoozing, opens an eye. "Ought to be chucked out."

I think sadly of poor *Middlemarch,* thrown away with the rubbish. Mum was so happy the day we found it. She said, "*Middlemarch!* I did that for A level. It's a wonderful book, Lol! You must read it when you're older."

I'm not chucking out a book that Mum wanted me to read. But for the moment I reluctantly agree that it can go up to the loft. It still makes me feel like I'm some kind of traitor. Like I'm committing cruelty to books. Mum's books are like *free range*. They're used to being out in the open, where books ought to be. Not shut away in the dark.

"Maybe they could go on the floor," I say, hopefully. I have visions of them lined up all the way round the room. But Holly looks outraged. She says, "This is where *Nan* sleeps when she stays."

I personally think it would be quite comforting, sleeping in a room full of books. When I have my own house I will have shelves of books going from floor to ceiling in every room. I try saying this to Holly, but she doesn't respond. She's pulled out Mum's Shakespeare that used to belong to Gran. She looks at the title – *Collected Works of William Shakespeare* – and pulls another face. "Don't want *that*."   Shakespeare is dumped on the bed next to *Middlemarch*. I can't help wondering what Mum would say. But the *Collected Works* are so big and fat they'd take up almost a quarter of the shelf. It wouldn't be fair on all the others.

Holly is tossing books like mad, thump thump thump, on to the bed. Mr Pooter curls up into a tight ball and tries to pretend it's not happening. I try too.

Thump. There goes another one. "Honestly! Is reading all you ever did?" says Holly.

I say no, of course not. But I'm thinking to myself

that it was one of the best things we ever did. I used to love curling up on the sofa, cuddling Mr Pooter, while Mum read to me.

"So what else did you do?" says Holly.

I say, "Lots of things."

"Like what?"

Like listening to music. Watching television. Playing Scrabble. Talking. Me and Mum used to talk all the time. But that isn't what Holly means. She means didn't we get out, and go places, like normal people. She thinks that me and Mum were seriously weird. She throws another book on to the bed.

"Didn't you have any friends, or anything?"

I hesitate. If I say no, she'll think I'm weirder than ever. Not that I really care what she thinks.

"You must have had some." She yanks out another book. "Who was your best friend?"

I mutter that I didn't have a best friend.

"Well, who did you hang out with?"

I hesitate again, then say, "Girl over the road."

"What was her name?"

"Temeeka." We didn't really hang out. We just used to play together when we were little.

"Was she an immigrant?" says Holly.

I frown and say, "Why?"

"It's a funny name."

"So what?"

Holly tosses another book on to the pile of rejects. "Mum says there's lots of them where you were. She says it made her feel like a stranger in her own land."

I point out that Auntie Ellen is Welsh, which means it's not her land anyway. Not if you're going to think like that. I don't, and neither did Mum, but I know that Auntie Ellen does. Was it rude of me to say about her being Welsh? Well, it doesn't matter; Holly doesn't get it. She's still going on about Temeeka and her funny name and whether she was an immigrant. She says, "*Was* she?"

I play for time, trying to make up my mind. I say, "Was she what?"

"Was she an immigrant!"

OK. I take a deep breath and say, "Yes, since you ask." It's a whopping great lie. I only said it to show that I wouldn't have *given a rap* even if she was. Holly rubs me up the wrong way, same as Auntie Ellen used to rub Mum. She's nodding now, looking smug and satisfied, like she's scored some sort of point. She picks up yet more books and lobs them on to the bed. In this really condescending voice she says that it must have been hard to make friends "living where you lived."

It wasn't anything to do with where we lived; it was cos of Mum not being well. At the end of school each day I used to rush home fast as I could, cos of knowing Mum would be there waiting for me. I'd call her when I was on my way, to see if we needed anything, then I'd stop off at the shop on the corner. Weekends I stayed in so we could be together. Even if I was invited to parties, though that didn't happen very often, I used to make excuses and say I couldn't go. I didn't tell Mum; I wouldn't have wanted her thinking she was holding me back. Cos she wasn't! It was my choice. I enjoyed being with Mum more than with anybody. If the weather was good we'd go up the park. I'd push Mum in her wheelchair and we'd go all the way round. Mum used to worry in case it was too much for me, but my arms are really strong. I could even push her uphill. There was that one time, though, when the chair tipped over going up a kerb and Mum nearly fell out. I was so ashamed! I feel ashamed even now, just thinking about it. How could I have let such a thing happen? To my own mum? Mum just giggled. She said, "You have to see the funny side of things!"

Mum always saw the funny side. It is what I try to do. It is just people like Holly and Auntie Ellen who make it so difficult.

Holly's still throwing books on to the bed. "Don't want that! Don't want that! This one's too big. Don't want big ones! Don't want—"

Quickly I say, "I want that one!"

"This one?" She looks at it, scornfully. "*Winnie-the-*

Pooh? You can't still be reading *Winnie-the-Pooh*! I grew out of that years ago."

I tell her that you can't grow out of *Winnie-the-Pooh*. Mum and me used to read it every Christmas. It was one of our traditions. "Anyway," I say, "it was a present."

"Who from?" She's peering inside, to see what's written there. "*To Lollipop, from Mum.*" Plus a row of kisses, but she doesn't read that bit. "Was that what she called you?"

"When I was little."

"*Lollipop.*" Holly giggles. "D'you know what I call you? The girl that laughed at the Queen!"

Mum and me *apologised* for that. And I wasn't laughing at the Queen, I was laughing at Mum pretending to be the Queen.

"*My husband and I...*" The words come shooting out of my mouth before I can stop them.

"You're doing it again!" Holly glares at me, accusingly. "You are such a rude person!"

I say that I'm sorry. I don't quite see what's rude

about it, just standing here in the bedroom, but I'm sure Mum would say I shouldn't have done it.

Holly slams *Winnie-the-Pooh* on to the shelf and dives back into the box. By the time she gets started on the last one I've managed to rescue thirty-five books, including *Little Women, Jane Eyre, David Copperfield, I Capture the Castle, Just William* and all of Jane Austen, cos she was Mum's favourite. Holly objects to *David Copperfield* on the grounds that he's the wrong size and looks untidy.

"He's too short and fat!"

For one wicked moment I'm almost tempted to say, "So are you!" But that would be *really* rude. And she isn't exactly fat, just plumped up like a pillow cos of Auntie Ellen letting her eat junk food all the time. I suppose, actually, she's quite pretty. She has this little round face with freckles, and her hair's bright red and curly. She gets her hair from Auntie Ellen. And the freckles. Uncle Mark is fair, like me and Mum. I'd rather be fair than ginger, but it would be nice, I think, to be curly instead of dead straight and limp. I toss back my ponytail and wrench *David Copperfield* away from her.

"He's staying!"

I put him on the shelf with the others. Holly, with an air of triumph, says that now I've only got room for one more. "You could have had two if you got rid of that fat one."

I say yes, well, I don't want two. I want *David Copperfield.*

"There's not many left anyway," says Holly. She burrows back into the box. *"War and Peace…* yuck! *Poetry.* Double yuck! *Diary of a Nobody.* Yuck yuck triple yuck! *Pil—"*

"Excuse me," I say, "I want that one."

"Which one?"

"Diary of a Nobody."

"What for?" She looks at it, suspiciously, like it might be something dirty.

"It's funny."

"Doesn't look funny."

"Well," I say, "it is."

"Why? What's it about?"

I tell her that it's about a man called Mr Pooter and his wife Carrie. "They've just moved into a new house and Mr Pooter's keeping a diary, all about the things that are happening to them."

"*Funny* things."

"Yes, and Mr Pooter keeps making these really bad jokes, like when he discovers his cuffs are frayed he says, *I'm 'fraid, my love, my cuffs are rather frayed.* And Carrie calls him a *spooney old thing.*"

"You think that's funny?" says Holly.

I have to admit it doesn't sound very funny. It did when Mum read it out, doing all the different voices. I try to think of a bit that doesn't need voices.

"One time he's doing some decorating and he's got this red paint left over, so he paints the bath? Then later on when he's lying there in the water the paint all comes off and he thinks he's burst an artery!"

Holly doesn't say anything; she just looks at me, like *you are seriously weird*. I know people think I'm weird. There was that girl at school, Alice Marshall, that I found crying in the girls' toilets one day, and when I asked her what the matter was she said nobody liked her and she didn't have any friends, so I said I'd be friends with her and she said what would be the point of that? "You're just weird!"

I suppose I must be, if everyone thinks I am. I never used to mind, once upon a time; I was happy just being me. Now I'm not so sure. I begin to have this feeling that it might be easier if I could somehow learn to be a bit more like other people. I really would like to be! But I don't seem to know how to do it.

I hold out my hand for the book. "Please," I say. "I have to keep that one."

Holly shrugs. "That's it then. The rest'll have to go. I'll tell Michael."

It's Michael who's going to take the boxes up to the loft. Into exile. Holly opens the door, then stops as something strikes her. "Is that why he's called Mr Pooter?" she says.

Mr Pooter twitches an ear at the sound of his name. I say yes, Mum called him that because he has a long beard, like Mr Pooter in the book. Well, long for a cat; cats don't usually have beards. But Mr Pooter is special. He has this lovely fringe of white fur all round his face.

"He's odd-looking," says Holly. "And he shouldn't be on your bed! It's not healthy, having cats in the bedroom. As for *that*—" She points an accusing finger at Mr Pooter's litter box, tucked away in the corner. "That's just disgusting!"

I tell her, indignantly, that it's clean as can be. "I empty it all the time!"

"Cats ought to go in the garden," says Holly.

"He can't, he's too old, and you haven't got a cat flap. Anyway, it's scary for him, a new place. He might get lost, or run over."

Holly doesn't actually *say* that she'd be glad if he did, but the truth is, nobody in this house likes cats. She grumbles that she doesn't know what's going to happen when her nan comes to say.

"You'll have to sleep in my room, and I'm not sleeping with cat poo! Not sleeping with a cat in the room, either. He'll have to go outside then."

I say in that case I'll go outside with him. "We'll both sleep in the kitchen."

"Then we'll have cat poo in the *kitchen*! That's even more disgusting. We'll all get poisoned!"

Stevie's never got poisoned. I wish I could have stayed and lived with Stevie! I'm sure it's what Mum would have wanted. But maybe Stevie wouldn't have liked it. In spite of being so good to Mum, she really only loves her cats.

Holly flounces off and I hear her thudding off down the stairs. I don't have the heart to begin cramming all the books back into their boxes. I throw myself on to the bed and rub my face in Mr Pooter's fur.

"It's all right," I whisper. "I won't let them put you out."

Mr Pooter gives a chirrup and stretches out an arm. He crimps a paw, then yawns and tucks his arm back again. I sit, cross-legged, beside him. What goes on in a cat's mind? Does Mr Pooter ever wonder where Mum has gone? Does he miss her? I'm sure he must, he was with her such a long time. Ever since he was a tiny kitten. But while he has me to look after him, he is safe. And he will *always have me*. That is a promise.

I'm still holding *Diary of a Nobody*. Mum and me were in the middle of reading it again; the bookmark's still in it. We'd got about halfway through. We were always reading *Diary of a Nobody*. I can't remember how old I was when Mum introduced me to it. I think I must have been about eight. Too young to properly enjoy it. Now I know it almost word for word. Mum did too. We both had our favourite bits that we waited for. One bit Mum specially loved was where Carrie and Mr Pooter send out for a bottle of Jackson Frères champagne whenever they feel like celebrating. It always got Mum giggling, so I used to giggle too, though I was never absolutely certain what I was giggling at. But whenever Mum and me wanted a treat, like at Christmas, for instance, or on Mum's birthday, she'd say, "Let's have some Jackson Frères!" Then after a while *everything* became Jackson Frères. A can of Coke, a glass of milk. Even just a glass of water. "Pass the Jackson Frères!" we'd go. It was like our private joke.

Michael has arrived. "Come to take the boxes up," he says.

I haven't even started packing them. I scramble guiltily off the bed.

"'s OK," says Michael. "I'll do it." Mr Pooter watches, carefully, as he starts collecting books. Michael looks at him. "Is he some kind of special breed?" he says.

I say no, he's just a common domestic short hair. That's what Stevie said.

"He looks like he's some kind of breed." Michael pats Mr Pooter on the head as if he's a dog. Mr Pooter lets him. He is *such* a good cat. "Pretty," says Michael. "Like sort of… dappled."

My heart swells with pride. Me and Mum always thought Mr Pooter was pretty.

"Like someone's spilt a can of orange paint over him."

"Or marmalade," I say.

"Yeah. Maybe he's a marmalade cat!"

Michael's busy, now, packing books. I'm handing them to him, one by one, and he's putting them in the boxes. He's not just stuffing them in all anyhow, like Holly would have done. He's stacking them neatly, in piles. Big ones at the bottom, small ones on top.

"This is a lot of books," he says. "I guess Auntie Sue was really into reading."

I tell him that Mum loved her books more than anything. "She always said books are what she'd rescue if the house ever caught fire. After Mr Pooter, of course. But once he was safe, she'd go back for her books."

I can see that Michael thinks it's strange, anyone rescuing books, but he's too polite to say so. He's like

Uncle Mark, he's really trying to be kind. He picks up a box and carries it to the door. It's obviously heavier than he'd thought.

"Don't reckon she'd have managed to rescue very many," he says.

Regretfully I say that I haven't, either. "There's not room."

"Maybe Dad could put up another shelf, only—" He stops. I know why he's stopped. It's because Auntie Ellen didn't want a shelf put up in the first place. This is where Holly's nan sleeps, and it's a tiny little room like a cupboard. It's why I wasn't allowed to bring Mum's bookcase. "Far too big," said Auntie Ellen. "Wouldn't fit in." It would if the wardrobe was taken out. I wouldn't care about not having a wardrobe. But Holly's nan probably expects it.

In this cheering-up kind of voice Michael says, "It's not like they're being got rid of. They're only up in the loft." He adds that he can always go up there and get a book down for me if there's one I specially want.

He is trying so hard. He really wants me to be happy. It ought to make things easier. Why does it make them worse?

"There's no problem," says Michael. "I'm up and down there all the time. Just let me know. OK?"

I seal up the chinks in my ice house wall.

"I will," says Ice Lolly, in her icicle tones. "Thank you."

Michael gives me this strange look. "By the way," he says, "next week—" Next week is when I'm starting back at school. The same school Michael goes to. "I just heard, you're going to be in my class."

I can't think what to say to this. I wonder if Michael wants me in his class, or whether I'll be an embarrassment. The girl who laughed at the Queen. Really *weird*.

Ice Lolly takes over. "That will be nice," she says.

Michael says, "Yeah…"

I feel almost sorry for him.

CHAPTER THREE

Today is Uncle Mark's birthday and we've all come into town, to the PizzaExpress. Where me and Mum lived, you could just walk up the road. Here, you have to drive. Auntie Ellen says it's healthier, being in the country, but it's not really country. Just lots of roads with fields on either side, only not the sort of fields you can walk in. Mostly they are full of cows and sheep and growing stuff. Corn, or something. I don't know much about it. Auntie Ellen says it's the ignorance of the town child. Uncle Mark says that I will get used to it. He says, "We'll always take you wherever you want to go." But I don't want to be taken! I want to go by myself. It's very worrying that I can't just walk to the library. What am I going to do about books? Maybe this new school will have some.

We've been shown to a table. I am sitting between Holly and Michael. Holly is studying the menu.

"Dad," she says, in wheedling tones, "can I have a starter *and* a main course *and* a pudding? Cos it's your birthday, Dad! And it's the big one, isn't it?" She cosies up to Uncle Mark. "It's the big one, Dad, isn't it?"

"It sure is," says Uncle Mark.

"*Forty*," says Holly. And then she goes, "Is that older or younger than Auntie Sue?"

Auntie Ellen says "Holly!" and frowns at her, but she can't ever take a hint. She has to keep on. "It's older, isn't it, Dad? Auntie Sue was your little sister." She turns to me.

"Don't you ever wish you had a sister?"

Michael gives her a thump. "Better off without, if you ask me," he says.

Holly screws up her face and sticks out her tongue. "Not if it means you're an only child. Only children get spoilt."

Did Mum spoil me? Auntie Ellen always says it was "unnatural", the way I was brought up, but it didn't feel unnatural to me. And I don't *think* I was spoilt. I know Mum never yelled at me or told me off, but that was because we used to talk about things. Like if I did anything she didn't like she'd make me sit down so we could discuss it. I don't call that being spoilt. Holly's more spoilt than I was. She only has to say she wants something and Auntie Ellen immediately buys it for her. She has *twenty pairs of shoes* in her wardrobe. She showed them to me. I only have two, and one of those is trainers.

Uncle Mark has decided he is going to order a bottle of wine, seeing as it's his birthday. Before I can stop myself I cry, "Jackson Frères!"

Everyone looks at me, including the waiter. They seem puzzled. They have obviously never read *Diary of a Nobody*. I say, "Jackson Frères… a bottle of Jackson Frères!"

Uncle Mark shakes his head, like *don't ask me*. "We'll just have the house white," he says.

"What's with all this Jackson Frères?" says Michael.

Suddenly, I don't want to talk about it. I wish I hadn't said it. It was our private joke, between me and Mum.

"Frère's French," says Holly. "Like *Frère Jacques*." She opens her mouth to start singing, but Uncle Michael cuts across her.

"What do you kids want? Coke?"

If Mum ever had wine, then I was always allowed a glass, too. But I know if I say so Auntie Ellen will only suck in her breath and that will be another black mark against Mum.

"Three Cokes," says Uncle Mark. Then he smiles at me and says, "So, Laurel! All set up for tomorrow?"

Tomorrow is the day I'm starting at this new school.

Bennington High. It has a black uniform. Auntie Ellen has dyed my old green skirt, but she had to take me into Asda to buy a black blazer and a black sweater. The only nice thing is the badge, which is red.

"Feeling OK about it?" says Uncle Mark.

I don't say anything; I just nod.

"She'll be all right," says Auntie Ellen. "She has Michael to look out for her. And it's a good school! Far better than where she was before."

What does Auntie Ellen know about where I was before?

"It's smaller, for a start," she says, "and not so mixed."

"Is mixed bad?" I say.

"It is if you're in the minority. Some of these inner city schools… hardly hear a word of English one day to the next, all the babble going on."

Earnestly I assure her that it only sounds like babble just at first. "You get used to it. You start learning other people's languages. Like I can say hello in French and Polish—" I check them off on my fingers, "and Greek and

Turkish and Gujarati and Russian and—"

"Yes, and you probably weren't allowed to celebrate Christmas," snaps Auntie Ellen.

"We did! We celebrated everything. Christmas, and Diwali, and Hanukkah, and—"

"Well, you won't have any of that here," says Auntie Ellen.

I stare at her, doubtfully. She makes it sound like a good thing. I don't think it's a good thing! "Are you a racist?" I say. I think she might be, but unless I ask I won't know.

Auntie Ellen grows red. I have made her angry. "What kind of a question is that?" she says.

Uncle Mark is also angry. "Laurel, that was quite uncalled for," he says. "Apologise to your aunt this instant!"

I'm confused. I wasn't being rude; I was just interested. I thought it was something we could discuss. But I say that I'm sorry, as it's probably what Mum would want me to do. Auntie Ellen, tight-lipped, pours herself a glass of water.

"This is the problem," she says, "when people are brought up without any kind of belief system."

"She doesn't believe in God," shrills Holly. "She told me so! She says he's just made up, like Father Christmas."

A little boy at the next table springs round with his mouth open. Auntie Ellen tells Holly to be quiet.

"She hasn't got a Bible," says Holly. "All those books and she hasn't even got a *Bible*!"

I say that we did have one, once. "I can't remember what happened to it. But Mum used to read me bits." I want them to know that Mum did do *some* things they would approve of. "She said they were good stories and the language was beautiful."

"*Stories?*" shrieks Holly. She shoots a glance at Auntie Ellen. "She thinks they're just stories!"

"Holly, hush," says Auntie Ellen. "It's not Laurel's fault. It's the way she was brought up."

I busy myself with the menu, trying to decide what to eat. I'm not really hungry. I wish I wasn't here! I wish they'd left me at home with Mr Pooter. It seems whatever

Mum did was wrong. Like whatever I do, like asking Auntie Ellen if she was a racist. We are always in disgrace.

We get back home at eight o'clock. Michael goes off to play one of his video games, while Uncle Mark and Auntie Ellen and Holly sit down to watch television. Uncle Mark asks me if I'm going to join them, but I say no, I'm going to go upstairs and pack my bag ready for tomorrow.

"Good idea," says Auntie Ellen. "Make sure you've got everything."

I come upstairs, but I don't pack my bag. There's nothing to pack. I already have my pencil case and stuff from before, and what else is there? Nothing, until I get given some books.

Mr Pooter chirrups and rolls over for me to tickle his tummy. I see that he's been a bit sick on the duvet and I clean it up, quickly, and turn the duvet over so that the wet bit is inside. I don't want Auntie Ellen catching sight of it. Cat people, like me and Mum and Stevie, know that these things happen; but Auntie Ellen is not a cat person.

She would say it is disgusting and unhygienic and that cats should not be in bedrooms.

I snuggle down next to Mr Pooter and pick up *Diary of a Nobody*. I think that I will continue to read it, starting from where me and Mum left off.

A beautiful day. Looking forward to tomorrow. Carrie bought a parasol about five feet long. I told her it was ridiculous. She said, "Mrs James of Sutton has one twice as long." So the matter dropped.

I'm reading the same few sentences over and over. I keep hearing Mum's voice, *Mrs James of Sutton has one twice as long.* When she was being Carrie, Mum put on this little funny fluttery voice that made me giggle. When she was being Mr Pooter, it was lower and a bit nerdy, and when she was being Lupin, Mr Pooter's son, it was all bold and brash.

Maybe it would be better to find a book that me and Mum have never read together. Except that I can't, because they're all up in the loft. I don't know what I'm going to do.

I close *Diary of a Nobody*. I leave the bookmark in there, in case one day I go back to it. There's some writing at the front; I've read it loads of times. It says, *To Sue, with all my love, Andi. I hope you find this little book as funny and delightful as I do!* I once asked Mum who Andi was. She said, "Someone from my youth." But she didn't tell me who and I never thought to ask again. I wish I had! Now I'll never know. I bet it was a boyfriend she used to have before she met the man that became my dad. I can't help thinking it's a pity she didn't marry him. I'm sure he would have made her a lot happier. But then, of course, she wouldn't have had me, she would have had someone totally different. That is quite scary; I would rather not think about it.

I put *Diary of a Nobody* back on the shelf and pick up Blue Bunny, instead. Blue Bunny is old and tatty, and I know I am past the age for soft toys, but he has been with me ever since I can remember. I take him on to the bed and cuddle up with him and Mr Pooter. There's a knock at the door and Holly comes in. She doesn't wait to be invited. She thinks it's enough just to knock.

She says, "Dad wants to know if you're going to come downstairs."

I say no, it's all right, I'd rather stay up here with Mr Pooter.

"I expect you could bring him down," says Holly, "if you wanted. So long as he doesn't get on the furniture. Or scrape things."

I say he doesn't scrape things any more. "He's too old for that."

"Seems like he's too old for anything," says Holly. "I think you ought to come down. Dad says it's not good for you to be up here by yourself. He says you need company. He's worried about you."

I ask her what he's worried about, and she says it's because I haven't cried. "If I lost my mum I'd cry buckets! It's only natural."

Natural for her; not for Ice Lolly. Mum would understand.

"Why don't you go and live with your dad, anyway?"

She throws it at me, accusingly, like it's my fault I've come here, cluttering up her nan's bedroom. "Wouldn't you rather live with your dad?"

I explain that nobody knows where my dad is, and I wouldn't want to live with him anyway. He made Mum so unhappy! He was horrid to her. It was when she was starting to get sick and she kept dropping things and breaking things and tripping over, and he used to yell at her and ask her why she had to be so clumsy.

"There's a girl in my class whose dad ran away," says Holly. "She cried for days. Did you cry when yours went?"

I don't really remember, but I don't believe I did. I think probably I was just relieved that he wasn't there to upset Mum any more.

"*Didn't* you?" says Holly.

I mutter that I might have done, but she's giving me that look that says, *you are just so weird.* I place Blue Bunny between Mr Pooter's paws. Holly hovers in the doorway.

"Did you get your bag packed?" she says. "Cos Dad doesn't like to be kept waiting in the morning."

I tell her that my bag is all ready.

Holly says, "Good." Then she says, "Mum's hoping you'll manage to find someone to make friends with. She says you can't rely on Michael all the time. He's a boy and he has friends of his own. She's scared you might get clingy or embarrass him, carrying on about how you don't believe in God and stuff."

I tell Holly that I won't say another word.

"Cos it's not clever," says Holly. "It doesn't impress people. And it's probably not believing in him that makes all these bad things happen."

I don't ask her what bad things; I don't want to know. I just want her to go away.

Still she hovers. "So are you coming," she says, "or not?"

I shake my head and clutch at Blue Bunny.

"You ought to put that thing in the washing machine," says Holly. "Or get rid of it. It's filthy!"

Finally, she's gone. I curl up again on the bed, stroking Mr Pooter with one hand and clutching Blue Bunny in the other. I'm not putting him in the washing machine! He might come to pieces. He's very old. Almost as old as I am. I have this memory of a lady giving him to me. I don't know who the lady was, but I remember I sat on her lap and she kissed me and hugged me. My dad was still there in those days, and after the lady had gone he and Mum had a fight. Dad shouted and Mum cried, and I got scared and hid behind the sofa. I remember that. I don't know what they fought about, but I think maybe it was something to do with the lady. I never saw her again.

I put Blue Bunny next to Mr Pooter and get them cuddling. Mr Pooter purrs, and crimps his paws. He likes Blue Bunny. Once, a few years ago, when Stevie wanted stuff she could sell to help the local animal charity, I told her she could have Blue Bunny. Mum was horrified. She said, "Lol, no! You can't give Bunny away, he's part of your past." So were lots of other things, but she didn't mind me giving them. She didn't even mind giving the crystal vase that had been one of her wedding presents. When I was little she always told me not to touch it because it was worth a lot of money. Then she went and gave it away. She said, "It's only an object. Just a bit more clutter. I'd sooner it went to the animals." But she wouldn't let me give Blue Bunny!

I'm glad, now. I think it's important to have things from your past.

There's another knock at the door. *Please* not Holly back again.

"Laurel?" It's Auntie Ellen's voice. "May I come in?"

I wish I could say no, but of course I can't. I make a mumbling sound, and the door opens.

"Holly tells me your bag's all packed and ready. Good girl!" Auntie Ellen comes over and sits on the edge of the bed. Mr Pooter immediately rolls on to his back, inviting a tummy rub, but she takes no notice. "Laurel," she says, "I know it's very difficult for you just at the moment. I know you're probably not looking forward to tomorrow, having to start at a new school in the middle of term, but—"

"It's all right." I sit up, very stiff and straight. "I won't cling. And I won't talk about God, I promise!"

Auntie Ellen's face turns slowly red. Not red because she's angry, like in the restaurant, but more like red because I've given away a secret. Holly wasn't supposed to have told me.

"Now, look," says Auntie Ellen, "I didn't say that. It's just that I'm worried about you. I'm worried that you may find it difficult to make friends. I don't think you're really used to having any, and some of the things you come out with… they don't help."

It's not clever. That's what Holly said. But I don't say them to be clever!

Auntie Ellen straightens the duvet. "It's a pity you're not still at primary school. It's easier there, and you'd be with Holly. Michael will look out for you, of course he will, but—"

"I won't embarrass him!"

I get it out quickly, before she can say it herself. Now she's redder than ever.

"Well," she says, "I'm sure you don't mean to. It's the

way you've been brought up. Just you and your mum, and that old woman. Stella, Stevie, whatever her name was. You don't seem…" She hesitates. I sit, looking at her. Waiting. "I don't know!" Auntie Ellen waves a hand. "You don't seem able to relate, somehow. There's Holly going out of her way to make you welcome, helping you unpack, and everything… Michael taking all those books up to the loft for you. They're doing their best! It's not easy for them, either. If you could just come halfway to meet them—"

I gaze down at Mr Pooter, who's gone back to sleep with Blue Bunny between his paws.

"The problem is, of course," says Auntie Ellen, "you've never been properly socialised. Shut away with your mum all the time… it wasn't natural."

I wasn't always shut away with Mum; only after she got sick. She needed me! There wasn't anyone else. Only Stevie, and she couldn't be there all the time. It used to worry Mum so much. She said to me once, "Oh, Lol, I never wanted it to be like this!"

It wasn't, to begin with. I can still remember, when I was little, how I used to have birthday parties. We used to have special treasure hunts, all round the house. Mum used to spend days working out the clues and hiding presents. I used to invite all the girls in my class, and they always, always came. All of them.

Mum tried ever so hard to keep going. It was just, in the end, it got too much. She didn't have the energy. It wasn't her fault!

Auntie Ellen can obviously read my thoughts. "I'm not blaming your mum," she says. "It's just the way things were. But you have to make an effort, Laurel. It's up to you. Anyway." Auntie Ellen stands up. "Now that you've packed your bag, how about coming downstairs to join the rest of us?"

I know that I have to make an effort. Auntie Ellen is making one, even though she'd probably rather not. I would also rather not! I desperately don't want to. But I can hear Mum's voice. She sounds so sad.

"Come on, Lol," she says. "Don't let me down. Fair's fair! Your aunt is doing her best."

With a little sigh, I slide off the bed and hoist Mr Pooter into my arms.

"Now why did you have to go and do that?" says Auntie Ellen. "Why disturb him? He was quite happy as he was."

I tell her that Mr Pooter likes to sit on my lap. "He always sits on my lap at night."

She makes an impatient clicking sound with her tongue. "Oh, very well! Bring him if you must."

I go downstairs and sit on the sofa, cuddling Mr Pooter. We all look at the television. I'm not sure what it is that we're watching; I'm locked away, safe inside my ice house. Tomorrow I'm going to be at this new school. Smaller, and not so mixed.

"Is there a library?" I've said it before I can stop myself. Everyone turns to look at me.

"Is there a library where?" says Uncle Mark.

"At the school."

"You mean Bennington?" says Auntie Ellen. "Of course there is!"

"*All* schools have libraries," says Holly.

I know they do. It was a really dumb question! It's just that I am starting to feel a bit anxious.

Under cover of the television, Michael leans across and whispers, "It's OK, I'll show you."

I whisper back, "Thank you." I'd like to assure him that I won't talk about God or do anything embarrassing, but the television's gone all low, so I can't. But I decide it will probably be best if I keep very quiet at this new school. Otherwise, it seems, every time I open my mouth I go and say something stupid or something that offends people.

Ice Lolly makes a vow: she will speak only when spoken to.

CHAPTER FOUR

Friday morning. In the car on the way to school. I'm sitting in the back with Michael, Holly's in the front with Uncle Mark. She always has to go in the front. She says she gets sick, otherwise. I think I might get sick if it was a long journey as I'm not very used to travelling by car. I don't know what would happen in that case. I suppose

I would have to use a plastic bag, which would be totally disgusting.

Something else which is a little bit disgusting… there is a smell wafting up from my sweater. Mr Pooter was sleeping on it during the night and brought up a bit of yellow stuff. I thought I'd got it all off, but there must be some I missed. I quiver my nostrils, trying to sniff the air without making it obvious what I'm doing. Michael doesn't seem to have noticed, so maybe I'm just imagining it. I think Mr Pooter must have made himself a nest because my sweater was all scrumpled and catty-smelling. He dribbles quite a lot. He can't help it. It is what old cats do.

"So!" That is Uncle Mark, booming out from the front of the car. "How are you getting on, Laurel?"

For a minute I think he means how am I getting on with my sweater, searching for bits of bile I may have missed. *Bile*. That is what the yellow stuff is called. But of course it is not what he means at all. He is talking about school.

"Made any friends yet?"

I have been at this school for two weeks, now. If I were Holly, I would probably have made a whole gang of friends. But you can't make friends unless you talk to people, and I am scared that if I open my mouth something inappropriate will come out. It is what Auntie Ellen accuses me of. *Making inappropriate remarks.* She says, "You really must think before you speak, Laurel."

So I am thinking how to answer Uncle Mark's question, but I take so long that in the end he gives up.

"Maybe on your birthday," he says, "you can invite some of your classmates for a pizza. When is your birthday? End of July, isn't it?"

That is weeks and weeks away. He is saying to himself that surely by then she will have made friends. I have made *one* friend. Mrs Caton, in the library. I know I am her friend because she has made me a library assistant and told me I can go into the library whenever I want and she will always be there if I want to talk. I don't worry about making inappropriate remarks when I'm with Mrs Caton. She is a book person, like me! But she is not the sort of friend that Uncle Mark is thinking of, which is why I don't mention her. He would say that a grown-up doesn't count. I am supposed to be making friends of my own age.

"Anyway," he says, "I don't imagine you're having any problems with your actual school work?"

Michael answers for me. "No," he says, "she's one of the clever ones."

Holly contorts her face and makes a vomiting sound. Michael tells her to shut up. "What do you know about anything, pea brain?"

Uncle Mark says that he would expect me to do well. "You take after your mum. She was always the bright spark of the family. First one to make uni!"

Jealously, Holly says, "I bet you could have gone if you'd wanted."

"Not without a struggle," says Uncle Mark. "I wasn't that way inclined. But your mum, Laurel…

she just flew through everything!"

I glow when he says that about Mum. And I love that I take after her! Not that I fly through everything, and I don't really think Mum did, either, cos we always used to giggle about how she still had to add up on her fingers.

"Well, OK," says Uncle Mark, "so what's happening today? What's on the menu?"

"Friday, fish and chips! Yum yum," says Holly.

"He doesn't mean food, stupid," says Michael. "He means lessons."

Holly turns pink. "Then why doesn't he say so?"

Uncle Mark explains that he was trying to be funny. "In a pathetic kind of way."

"Menu means *food*," says Holly, all self-righteous. "*Timetable* means lessons."

Uncle Mark groans. "All right, I give in! What's on the timetable?"

Michael rattles through it. "Maths, history, English… hey!" He nudges at me. "Your turn to read!" He tells

Uncle Mark how Mr Tinsley always has someone read a passage from one of their favourite books for the last ten minutes of double English. Today it's going to be me. I've been looking forward to it all week.

"Sounds right up your street," says Uncle Mark. "What book have you chosen?"

He's talking to me, so I have to answer, though for some reason I find that I suddenly don't want to. Reluctantly, I say that I'm going to read from *Diary of a Nobody*.

"*Diary of a Nobody?* Never heard of that one," says Uncle Mark. "What's it about?"

Holly shrills out from the front seat. "It's about some boring old man writing his diary!"

"A children's book?" Uncle Mark sounds surprised. "Whatever happened to *Harry Potter*?"

"We had *Harry Potter* last week," says Michael. "Lots of people did it."

"So what are you doing when it's your turn?"

Michael says he's going to read something from a book about the ancient Egyptians. "Mummies, and stuff."

"More interesting than boring old men writing their stupid diaries," says Holly.

I knew there was a reason I didn't want to tell Uncle Mark. I wish, now, that I hadn't chosen *Diary of a Nobody*. I was going to do it with all Mum's different voices, but suppose people just think I'm showing off? I realise that I've made another of my mistakes. I'm always making mistakes. Like my inappropriate remarks. Maybe I can go to the library at lunchtime and find something else. I don't want one of Mum's favourite books being sneered at!

Period I on a Friday is maths. It's not one of my best subjects, though I'm better at it than Mum was. At least I don't have to use my fingers! When we went shopping together, Mum always gave me the job of adding the prices and checking the change. But next year, when we're put into different sets, I don't think I'll be in the top one. Not for maths. I will for French and English, and maybe history and geography. And Spanish, if I do it. If I'm still here. I suppose I will be. I can't think of any reason I'd be anywhere else.

For a moment, as I unpack my bag and take out my maths books, I desperately wish I was back at Gospel Road. I don't care what Auntie Ellen says about this school being better, and smaller, and not so mixed, I'd got used to where I was. I think maybe I am not very good at coping with change. I am not a very adventurous sort of person.

I gaze round at the rest of the class. It is hardly mixed at all. Almost everybody is English. Maybe *everybody*. There are two black kids and a few Asians, but they are all English. They all *speak* English. They were all born here. At Gospel Road, people came from everywhere. All over the world. I am scared I shall forget how to say hello in all those different languages. I can remember French and German; they're easy. *Bienvenue* and *willkommen*. And Spanish and Italian. *Bienvenido, benvenuto*. But I can't remember Urdu or

Gujarati! And Polish and Turkish. They are all disappearing, cos I don't hear them any more and there's no one I can ask. At Gospel Road we had them written out and stuck on the classroom doors. They don't do that here.

I'm squeezing my eyes tight shut, trying to visualise some of the words and see if it will jog my memory. Suddenly I hear the voice of Mr Gurney, telling Carla Phillips that he's not having her and Maisie Thompson sitting together any more.

"You're here to learn maths, not fritter away your time painting your nails and doing each other's hair. Maisie, change places with Tiffany. And Carla, you can come down here and sit next to Laurel. I want you where I can see you."

My heart sinks. Carla's like the class bad girl. Does whatever she pleases. I sort of admire her, in a way, though I don't really like her. She probably doesn't like me, either. If she's ever noticed that I'm here, which she may not have done.

Mr Gurney says, "Well, come along, come along! We haven't got all day."

Carla snatches up her bag and comes banging resentfully down the aisle, crashing into desks as she goes. She lets herself fall with a big THUMP into the seat next to mine. My pen bounces off the top of the desk and I bend down to get it. On the way back up I catch Carla's eye. She glares at me and curls her lip. I feel like saying, "It's not my fault," but that would just make her even madder. Maybe she thinks it is my fault. If I hadn't been sitting by myself, Mr Gurney might not have moved her down here in the first place. She's incredibly angry. All huffing and puffing and slamming things about. Mr Gurney ignores her and starts drawing triangles all over the board. I do my best to concentrate, though it's difficult with Carla behaving like some kind of hurricane.

After a few minutes she stops all her frenzied activity and starts sniffing the air. She leans in towards me and sniffs again. Then she makes a noise like

"Yeeuurgh!" and catapults away from me, clapping her hand dramatically across her face. Mr Gurney spins round.

"Now what's the problem?" he says.

In muffled tones, from behind her hand, Carla announces that she's being gassed.

"What are you talking about?" says Mr Gurney.

Carla pegs her nose between finger and thumb. "There's a *smell*."

Now everyone's sniffing. Mr Gurney snaps, "Live with it!"

"But it's disgusting! It's like stale sick."

"Too bad," says Mr Gurney. "Just settle down, settle down!"

Mr Gurney goes back to his triangles. Carla, with a flounce, moves her chair into the gangway and sits with her back towards me. I think very hard of Mr Pooter. Poor little old cat, it's not his fault. Mum always said what a clean boy he was. He used to spend hours grooming himself; he doesn't do it any more. I'll have to brush him. And clip his nails. Stevie told me I must make sure they don't grow too long, now that he can't do these things for himself. She even gave me a special pair of clippers and showed me how to use them.

I look venomously at Carla's back, trying to picture her as an old woman, unable to look after herself. I see her all warty and gnarled and people holding their noses and complaining that she smells. It makes me feel a bit better.

At the end of class Carla turns to me and says, "Don't you ever wash?"

I don't say anything. I'm not going to tell her about Mr Pooter, she might say something unkind.

"Honestly, you *stink*." She wafts the air. Other people gather round. Their noses twitch.

"What is it?" says Maisie.

"Whatever it is," Carla hooks her arm through Maisie's as they go off together, "it's repugnant."

How does she know a word like that? Even I don't know it. Repugnant, repugnant. It's obviously something unpleasant. Something to do with smells. I make a mental note to find out.

Next lesson is PE and a girl called Luisa complains that she doesn't want my clothes hanging anywhere near hers, so I bundle them up and leave them in a heap and then get into trouble from Mrs Eaton for not hanging them on a peg. Luisa tells me that she's sorry, but, "You do smell."

Now it's lunch, which I eat by myself. No one wants to sit next to me on account of my being so repugnant. Afterwards I go into the girls' cloakroom and try soaking bits of toilet paper and using it to sponge myself, but the toilet paper just crumbles and leaves bits like confetti all over my sweater, so now I'm wet as well as repugnant. I am beginning to understand why it was that Stevie always had a bit of a smell attached to her.

In desperation I take the sweater off and stuff it into my bag. My blouse is all crumpled and creased from being under Mr Pooter all night, but it doesn't have any yellow stains on it so it is not quite as repugnant.

I go upstairs to the library and immediately start to feel happier. Down at the far end the library is full of people working on the computers, but here at the books end it is mainly just me and Mrs Caton. She is really pleased to see me.

"Oh, Laurel," she says, "I'm so glad you've come! There's a whole load of books that need putting away and neither of the others has turned up."

She means the other two library assistants. They are simply not reliable.

"What would I do without you?" she says, as I start shelving books.

I don't honestly think she would be able to manage. Not only do the others not always turn up, but sometimes they put books back in the wrong places.

I ask Mrs Caton if she knows what the word repugnant means. She says, "Disgusting, maybe? If that makes sense. How was it used?"

Even though she is my friend, I can't bring myself to tell her. It is too shameful. But I say that it makes sense.

"It's an unusual word," she says. Then she smiles and says, "You like unusual words, don't you?"

I'm so pleased she's noticed. Me and Mum were always on the lookout for new words. I tell Mrs Caton that just the other day I discovered a really good one: *seersucker*. I tell her how I looked it up in the dictionary and what it meas. It means a sort of thin cloth that comes from India.

"I think it's such a lovely word... seersucker! Only it doesn't *sound* like cloth, it sounds like something you'd say to someone if they were being stupid, like you might say, *Oh, don't be such a seersucker!* Cos words don't always mean what you'd think they'd mean, do they?"

Mrs Caton agrees that they don't. She asks me what I've chosen as my favourite book to read from in English this afternoon.

I say that I *had* been going to read from *Diary of a Nobody*. "Do you know *Diary of a Nobody*? It's a grown-up book, not a children's one. It's really funny! It's all about this man, Mr Pooter, that's writing his diary. He keeps making these terrible jokes, like *I'm 'fraid, my love, my cuffs are rather frayed*, so that everyone goes *groan*. And then there's his wife, she's called Carrie. She says he's a *spooney old thing*. And he's got this son, Lupin, who causes him lots of trouble. He gets in a real state about Lupin, cos of Lupin not having any respect. Mr Pooter's got respect. Like at work, there's his boss, Mr Perkupp. And Mr Pooter says *You are a good man, Mr Perkupp*, and all the young boys that work in the office start laughing at him, cos they haven't got any respect either. You ought to read it," I say.

"I will, I will," says Mrs Caton. "Unfortunately, I don't think we have it on the shelves, but—"

I thrust my hand into my bag. "I could lend you it to you, if you like."

"No, really, Laurel, I'll look for it in the public library. They're bound to have it."

"But I've got it right here!" I'm eager for her to read it, so we can talk about it together. But Mrs Caton says

PETERBOROUGH PUBLIC LIBRARY

quite honestly, just at the moment, she doesn't have the time.

"I'm completely snowed under! But I will read it, I promise you. It sounds like fun."

"There's this lovely bit," I say, "where Mr Pooter paints the bath with red paint." I flick through the pages, trying to find it. "He goes to have a bath and it all comes off all over him and—"

And then I have to stop, because a Year 7 butts in wanting to know where she can find the Woodland Fairies books. I know the library is for everyone, but I really hate it when my conversations with Mrs Caton are interrupted, specially when it's people asking silly questions about silly books. What's a Year 7 doing, still reading Woodland Fairies? And why can't she go and find them for herself?

It's wrong to think like that. Mum would say it's better to be reading Woodland Fairies than not reading at all, and that everyone needs to be encouraged. I know this! It's just that my moments in the library are the best moments of the day. Me and Mrs Caton always have so much to talk about!

Mrs Caton goes off in search of fairies and I continue flicking through the pages of *Diary of a Nobody*.

"I've got it!" I cry, as Mrs Caton comes back with the Year 7 and her fairy book. "This is where he's in the bath. He says—"

"Oh, now, Laurel, don't ruin it for me!" Mrs Caton holds up a hand, like a policeman stopping the traffic. "Let me discover it for myself. There you are, Amy."

The Year 7 scuttles off with her book. I put *Diary of a Nobody* back in my bag.

"Anyway," I say, "I've changed my mind. I'm going to read something else, but I can't quite decide what." I lean across the desk, fiddling with the date stamp. I'm looking forward to a long cosy discussion about books, and which one I should read, but before we can even get started the telephone's gone and rung and Mrs Caton's answering it. Of course I know she has to. I peel myself off the desk and wander about amongst the shelves, looking for something to read. I come across *Jane Eyre*. I could read *Jane Eyre*! The bit at the beginning, where she's locked in the red-room. I always used to find that really scary.

I gallop back, triumphantly, to get the book checked out.

"Oh, yes," says Mrs Caton. "*Jane Eyre*… one of my favourites!"

I tell her that I'm going to read the bit where Jane is locked away in the red-room.

"It's really scary! Did you find it really scary? When you were young? Did you read it when you were young? I read it when I was ten years old. Well, Mum read it to me. I didn't understand quite all of it, but—"

"Laurel, that was the bell," says Mrs Caton. "You'd better go, or you'll be late for class." She hands me back *Jane Eyre*, and reluctantly I take it. I would stay here in the library all day, if I could. "Have a nice weekend," says Mrs Caton. "I'll see you on Monday."

It seems a long time to wait. We'll have loads to talk

about by then! I'm never at a loss for words with Mrs Caton, but I can't help being a bit relieved, now, that I didn't lend her Mum's copy of *Diary of a Nobody*. I want her to read it, but suppose something happened, like she left it on a bus or dropped it in the bath? I know she would buy me another copy, but it wouldn't be the same. This one still has Mum's touch on it. And besides, it was given to her by Andi. I'm sure he must have been someone Mum was in love with.

At the end of English, I go to the front of the class and read my page from *Jane Eyre*. When I've finished reading, Mr Tinsley says, "All right! Who has any comments?"

There's a silence; then Michael puts up his hand. He says he thought the bit I read was quite interesting, but it wouldn't actually make him want to go and read the book. When Mr Tinsley says why not, Michael says he doesn't know. "It just wouldn't."

A boy called Todd Masters yells, "Too girly!" and everyone laughs, except me and Mr Tinsley.

"Well, if you want to know what I think," says Mr Tinsley, "I think it was an excellent choice and beautifully read. Well done, Laurel! I'm glad there's still someone who's prepared to read the classics."

I try not to be smug, though it's hard not to feel just a little bit pleased. Maybe I *look* smug, even though I don't mean to. Or maybe it's just that Carla's still mad at me after this morning, being forced to sit by me. As soon as the bell's rung for the end of class, and Mr Tinsley's left the room, she plants herself before me and goes, "Hey, Stinky! Jane *Eyre*. Excellent *choice*. Trust you!"

I don't understand what she means, trust me. What have I done now?

Michael suddenly steps forward. "Don't talk to her like that," he says. "She's just lost her mum."

There's this long, uneasy silence. Then Carla recovers herself.

"Yeah, well," she says. "Sorry."

"That's all right. I'm an android."

I freeze. I can't believe that's my voice speaking. Why

does it keep doing this? Why can't it just be quiet? They're all looking at me, like I'm mad.

"What's she talking about?" says Carla. "What's an android?"

One of the boys says it's like a robot.

"You mean, like a Dalek or something?"

Not like a Dalek. Like a robot in human form. Androids can do everything that human beings can do. They just don't feel anything. Like ice lollies.

As we leave school at the end of the afternoon, Carla shouts, "Bye, Dalek!"

Maybe it will become my nickname. Mum had a nickname when she was at school. It was Wally, because of her surname being Walters. And then she got married and became Winton. I don't care if people want to call me Dalek. It doesn't matter to me what I'm called.

I think over the weekend I will make up a new diary entry for Mr Pooter. Mrs Caton would enjoy that.

CHAPTER FIVE

"*This morning Carrie went to visit her friend Mrs James of Sutton. While she was away—*"

It's Monday, lunchtime. I'm in the library, reading my diary entry to Mrs Caton.

"*While she was away I found a big tin of yellow paint in the cellar. It seemed a good opportunity to redecorate the front*" *parlour, which has marks down one of the walls where Lupin scraped it while moving a piece of furniture.* Lupin is Mr Pooter's son," I explain.

"I see." Mrs Caton nods. "Jolene, could you make a start on putting those books away. And Maria, maybe you could see to the magazines. Put all the old ones in the cupboard. Yes, go on, Laurel. Lupin is Mr Pooter's son—"

I say, "Yes, and he is a sore trial to him. Anyway." I continue with my reading. "*By the time Carrie was due back I had painted the entire room. I had even painted the floorb*—"

"Just a second, Laurel! Yes, Tom. What can I do for you?"

I wait, patiently, while Mrs Caton sorts out a problem with a book. Before she's finished, someone else comes in with another problem. Why can't they sort these things out for themselves? I would!

"*The floorboards,*" I say – and immediately have to stop again. This time it's Jolene, wanting to know whether Elinor M. Brent-Dyer goes under B or D. She should have learnt by now!

"Right," says Mrs Caton. She turns back to me. "Where had we got to? He's painted the room—"

"And he says, *I thought it looked very bright and cheery and felt sure Carrie would agree with me. As soon as I heard her key in the door—*"

"Over there," says Mrs Caton, pointing to the magazine cupboard.

"*I went into the hall to meet her, saying, 'Did you have a good day, my love? I am glad to see you back as I have a nice surprise for you. Pray go and—*"

"It's locked!" cries Maria. "It won't open!"

The cupboard isn't locked; it's just a bit stiff. I say, "Tug it!" and she tugs, and all the magazines come spilling out on to the floor. That is because they were not put away properly to begin with. Mrs Caton goes over to help clear the mess. I trail after her, still reading. I've reached the bit where Carrie comes out of the parlour, screaming that there has been a terrible accident. "*I asked her—*"

"Excuse me, Laurel!" Mrs Caton is busy collecting up

magazines. "Can you just move a bit to your right? That's it, that's better."

I move away but go on reading. " ... *asked her what she meant, and she said, 'Someone has been monstrously sick all over the floor.' Oh, I did laugh! I thought that Carrie would also laugh when I explained to her that it was yellow paint, but I fear she has lost her sense of humour. She told me that she was not sure she wanted her parlour to look as though it was covered in sick. So now I have to go to all the trouble of re-doing it. A man's work,*" I finish up, triumphantly, "*is never done.*"

"And neither, it seems, is a librarian's," says Mrs Caton, stuffing magazines back into the cupboard. "Jolene! Easy Readers... down there! That was excellent, by the way, Laurel. It really makes me want to read the book."

I knew she would like it. I say maybe she could buy a copy for the library, and she says she will certainly think about it.

"Though I am not sure," she adds, "how many people would share your enthusiasm. You're obviously a very committed reader. But look," she says, as we go back to the desk, "I've got all the help I need today. Why don't you have a bit of a break and go outside in the sunshine?"

I tell her that I like being here, in the library.

"And I like having you here," says Mrs Caton. "But if we're not careful I shall get into trouble for overworking you! You don't want me to get into trouble, do you?"

I hesitate. I'm almost certain she's just joking. She has to be. I know that Jolene and Maria mean well and have to be encouraged, but I am the one Mrs Caton depends on. She said so herself! Where would she be without me?

"Laurel?" she says.

"I'll just go and sort out the magazines," I say. "Put them all in date order."

Mrs Caton sighs. "Well, all right," she says. "They could certainly do with it. But, Laurel—"

I wait, expectantly. Mrs Caton shakes her head. "Nothing," she says. "Don't worry. Go and see to the magazines."

* * *

At the end of the day, I go home with Michael. We have to use the bus on the way back. Usually I'm on my own, but today he is with me. We walk down to the main road to the bus stop and I tell him that I want to visit Tesco to buy some cat food for Mr Pooter.

"He doesn't like the dry stuff, he's not used to it."

Michael says his mum got the dry stuff specially. He sounds a bit hurt, like I'm criticising. "She thought it would be better… less messy. Save having to keep washing up cat bowls all the time."

I tell him that I would wash them up. I always did, at home. I did all the washing up. And the drying. And the putting away. Mum couldn't manage it, so I took over. I didn't mind.

We go into Tesco and I buy four tins of very expensive cat food. I can only afford four out of my pocket money. Michael seems to think I'm mad, spending all that on a mere cat. He doesn't *say* mere cat, but I know that is what he is thinking. He says why don't I get own brand? "It's probably just as good." I say that

Mr Pooter needs to be tempted. He hasn't been eating well just lately.

"That's probably cos he's old," says Michael. "I mean... how long can cats live?"

I don't want to think about how long cats can live.

"Fifteen?" says Michael.

Mr Pooter is sixteen. But Stevie had cats that lived to be twenty.

"There's nothing wrong with him," I say. "He just doesn't like dry food. It may be because of his teeth. This'll be easier for him."

"Well, you'd better not let Mum know," says Michael. "She wouldn't like the thought of you feeding him tinned stuff in your bedroom. She doesn't mind if it's dry, but not out of a tin."

"It's all right, he won't make a mess," I say. "He's a very clean cat."

Michael goes "Hm," like he doesn't believe a cat can be clean.

"I know your mum hates him," I say.

"She doesn't *hate* him. She just doesn't like having animals indoors."

"He can't live outdoors!"

"No, she wouldn't make him," says Michael. "She wouldn't be unkind, or anything. But she likes the place to look nice. She didn't have nice things when she was a girl. Nan and Grandad always had to struggle."

I think to myself that Mum and me had to struggle too, especially after Mum got ill. And we didn't have nice things, either; just each other, and Mr Pooter, and loads of books. It was all we needed, really.

"See, Mum and Dad," says Michael, "have worked hard to get where they are. It upsets them when things get spoilt. I guess it would upset anyone, unless they were millionaires."

I wonder what millionaires have to do with it.

"They could replace stuff," says Michael. "Mum and Dad can't. I don't suppose your mum could, either."

I agree that she couldn't. "But Mum didn't mind a bit of mess. She always said she'd rather have Mr Pooter and the odd furball or scratched chair than everything neat and clean and no cat to keep us company."

"I guess everyone's different," says Michael. And then, as we leave Tesco and start walking back to the bus stop, he says, "What did you mean the other day when you said you were an android?"

"I just…" My voice trails off; I don't know how to answer. How can I explain what I meant? I wish I'd never said it. "I just… it was just… an expression."

"Androids aren't human," says Michael. "D'you reckon you're not human?"

I stand at the bus stop, clutching my bag full of cat food tins. Slowly, I shake my head.

"They don't feel anything. D'you reckon you don't feel anything?"

I stay silent.

"Dad says you've closed up. He says that's not good."

I stare determinedly, straight ahead.

"Mum says it's your way of coping. She says if you want to talk, you'll talk, and if you don't, it's up to you. Anyway."

Michael sticks out his hand as the bus appears. "You feel something for Mr Pooter," he says, "so you can't be totally android."

We don't have much conversation as we sit on the bus. I look out of the window and Michael takes a magazine from his bag. As soon as we get home I race upstairs as usual and into my bedroom. Mr Pooter is waiting for me, on top of the wardrobe. I didn't know he could still jump that high. He chirrups at me, and I stand on a chair and very carefully lift him down. We roll on the bed together and he head butts me, purring and dribbling. Anxiously I scan the room, checking that he hasn't been sick anywhere. He hasn't! My heart lifts.

I fetch his feeding bowl and open one of the tins. Mr Pooter kneads the duvet, in anticipation. His claws have made tiny pinpricks, which I hope Auntie Ellen won't notice. I haven't got a spoon and I don't want to go down and get one in case someone sees me and asks what I want it for, so I squish stuff out with the end of my ruler.

"There," I say, putting the bowl in front of Mr Pooter. "Real kitty food!"

Mr Pooter gobbles it down. I knew it was the dry stuff he didn't like. You can't change an old cat's habits. I stroke him and tell him he's a good boy.

"You stay there," I say. "I'll get you some clean water."

I refill his water bowl in the bathroom, and wash the ruler. I don't know what to do with the cat tin, which is still half full. I can't put it in the fridge, Auntie Ellen would go ballistic. In the end I tear a page out of my maths book and fix it over the top of the tin with an elastic band, then I hide the tin at the back of the wardrobe. Fortunately the weather is not too hot, so I think it will keep all right for a couple of days. I put the other tins in with it.

I will have to go down, soon, for tea. Auntie Ellen is very strict like that; we all have to eat together, at the same time. We also have to sit up properly, at table, not just slob around like me and Mum, on the sofa.

I perch on the edge of the bed and tip up my bag. A shower of books falls out. My pencil case isn't done up properly and all the pens and pencils scatter across the duvet. While I'm scrabbling them up I see something white tucked down the back of the bag. I pull it out. It's a letter. It's addressed to Ms A. Stafford c/o Erudite Publishing Ltd, with PERSONAL and PLEASE FORWARD printed underneath in Mum's rather wobbly handwriting. She'd got so she couldn't hold a pen very well so usually she had me write things for her or do them on the computer (until it conked out).

I sit, clutching the envelope, thinking that I am holding it where Mum held it all those weeks ago. Cos I remember, now. She gave it to me that morning and asked me to buy a stamp and post it for her. She wasn't feeling very well and I didn't want to leave her. But Mum said she'd be all right, she said that Stevie would be looking in.

"She'll sit with me for a bit. You go on! I don't want you missing school."

So I went, but because I was late I didn't stop to buy a stamp; I jumped straight on to the bus. I slipped the letter into the pocket at the back of my bag, meaning to post it on my way home. But then halfway through the morning I was called out of class and and told that Mum had been taken to hospital, and when I got there I found Stevie waiting for me, and she said, "You're a few minutes too late," and after that the letter just went right out of my mind. It's been in my bag all this time.

I take a deep breath. I am Ice Lolly. I am an android. *Androids don't feel anything.*

Mr Pooter lands on my lap with a thump. Mechanically, I stroke him. I wonder who Ms A. Stafford is and who Erudite Publishing are. I wonder if the letter is important and whether I should read it. I think perhaps I ought; Mum was very anxious that I should post it. I start to slip a finger under the flap of the envelope to ease it open. Then I stop. Me and Mum never had secrets, but still it doesn't seem right to open one of her letters. Specially when it says PERSONAL. I think of Mum going to the trouble of spelling it out. I see her hunched over, trying to grip the pen, trying to keep her hand steady. I won't read the letter! I'll get a stamp from Uncle Mark and I'll put it in the box first thing tomorrow.

Holly bangs at the door and shouts that it's time for tea. I settle Mr Pooter on the bed and tell him I'll be back in a minute. I think that maybe after tea I might take him in the garden so he can get some air. I've been doing this lately; he likes to potter about, smelling the flowers. It gets Auntie Ellen a bit fussed in case he "does something". She means in case he goes to the toilet. But I have assured her that I will be very careful to clear up after him if he does. She says, "Just make sure that you do." She thinks there is nothing worse than someone's cat wandering into the garden and doing something.

Uncle Mark is home. I ask if I can have a stamp for a letter. He says, "Of course you can! First or second?"

I say please could it be first, and Auntie Ellen frowns. "What's wrong with second class?" she says.

I tell her that I've just discovered a letter I was supposed to post and never did. She says, "Oh, very well, then," but I know she isn't pleased. Lots of things I do don't please Auntie Ellen. Uncle Mark gives me a first-class stamp and I offer to pay for it, because I think this will make Auntie Ellen happy with me, but Uncle Mark tells me not to be so silly.

"What's a first-class stamp between friends?"

I'm not quite sure what this means, except that I don't seem to get on Uncle Mark's nerves the way I get on Auntie Ellen's. Maybe it's because Mum was his sister and he feels like I'm part of the family. Auntie Ellen doesn't feel that. Neither does Holly. They'd rather I wasn't here. I don't think Michael minds so much.

After tea, Uncle Mark goes out to his shed in the garden, where he makes things; Michael goes over the road to visit a friend; Holly and Auntie Ellen go into the other room and I go back upstairs to fetch Mr Pooter. To my horror, as I open the door I step in something: it's a pile of sick. Mr Pooter has brought up all his lovely dinner! He is crouched in the corner, looking sorry for himself. I want to go and cuddle him, and tell him it's all right, he hasn't done anything wrong, but in fact I am in a panic. The sick is on the carpet, and the carpet is pink. I must get rid of it! I must clean it up immediately, before Auntie Ellen sees.

I turn and rush back downstairs and into the kitchen, where I rip off sheet after sheet of kitchen roll. Then I grab a sponge from under the sink and tear back upstairs. Frantically I mop up the sick with the kitchen roll and dash along the landing with it and into the toilet, where I stuff it down the pan, a whole great wodge of it, and pull the chain. Next I soak the sponge in the bathroom basin and go whizzing back to clean the carpet. My heart is pounding. I expect Auntie Ellen to appear at any moment. I rub and I scrub until the sponge starts to break up and little bits of yellow go flaking all over the floor. It looks like confetti. And there is still a stain, which won't come out.

Desperately, I seize the flowered rug at the end of my bed. I am about to place it over the stain when I hear Holly's voice, shrieking hysterically.

"*Mu-u-u-u-um!*"

I drop the rug and go dashing out, on to the landing.

Holly is standing at the top of the stairs. I ask her what the matter is. She turns, wild-eyed.

"The toilet's overflowing! It's all full of kitchen roll!"

My heart goes plummeting, right down into the pit of my stomach. I rush to the toilet. Holly is right. Water is welling up, with masses of kitchen roll floating in it. I yank the chain, and more water wells up. It won't stop. It's starting to trickle out on to the floor.

"We're going to be flooded," moans Holly.

Auntie Ellen has arrived. She takes one look and goes, "Holly! Get your father."

Holly skitters off. Auntie Ellen snaps, "Laurel, don't just stand there! Go and get some rubber gloves."

I race down to the kitchen, snatch the gloves and gallop back up. Auntie Ellen pulls on the gloves and starts fishing out mounds of waterlogged kitchen roll and dumping them in the hand basin. The water level drops very slightly, but the water doesn't actually go away. Uncle Mark comes pounding along the landing, with Holly in tow.

"What's going on?"

"Someone," says Auntie Ellen, "has clogged the toilet. Who did it?" She whirls round on me and Holly. "Who was stupid enough to put kitchen roll in there?"

"It wasn't me!" shrills Holly.

"Laurel? Was it you?"

I mumble that I am very sorry. "I thought it would go away."

"Well, of course it won't just go away! It's far too thick. Mark, what are we going to do?"

"Try and unblock it," says Uncle Mark. "We need some kind of plunger… do we have a mop, or anything?"

Auntie Ellen says there's an old one in the kitchen cupboard. She tells Holly to go and fetch it. Holly scoots off again, and I stand, like I'm mesmerised, looking at the water.

"*Why* did you put kitchen roll in there, anyway?" says Auntie ellen.

"I—" I swallow. I daren't tell her about Mr Pooter. "I spilt something… I used kitchen roll to mop it up."

"Spilt what?" says Auntie Ellen; but at that moment Holly comes back with the mop and everyone's attention turns to Uncle Mark. We all watch as he stuffs the head of the mop into the toilet bowl and pumps up and down with it. I hear the water going *glob*. Please, I think, *please* let it go away!

But it doesn't. It gurgles and globs, but the level stays the same. Holly wails that she needs to use the toilet.

"I can't hold it!"

Michael, who is back indoors and has come upstairs to see what all the fuss is about, tells her to use the garden. Holly bawls, "I'm not using the garden. That's disgusting!"

"Be even more disgusting if you wet your knickers," says Michael.

Holly turns pink. Auntie Ellen tells Michael to leave his sister alone. "It's not her fault." Michael looks with interest at the soggy mounds of tissue in the basin.

"So who did it?"

"*She* did." Holly stabs a finger in my direction. "She went and stuffed kitchen roll down there."

"Cool," says Michael.

"It's not cool, you idiot!" Holly takes a swipe at him. "It's *stupid*!"

"It certainly will be stupid," says Uncle Mark, "if we have to get the drain people in… Michael, take over for a minute. I'll give them a ring and see what they charge."

Michael kneels by the side of the toilet and begins energetically pumping up and down. I think secretly he is quite enjoying it. But he does it so vigorously that water starts splashing over the floor and makes Auntie Ellen cross.

"You don't have to go mad," she says.

"Got to get it unblocked," pants Michael.

Uncle Mark comes back. He pulls a face. "Well," he says, "we can knock that idea on the head."

"Why?" says Auntie Ellen. "What did they say?"

"Emergency call out, this time of night… two hundred quid."

"*What?*"

"Two hundred quid."

"That's ridiculous!" Auntie Ellen turns on me. "This is all your doing!"

I hang my head. Uncle Mark takes back the mop and begins plunging again. Holly clutches at herself and whines.

"Oh, go downstairs and do what your brother says!" snarls Auntie Ellen. "For goodness' sake!"

Holly goes grizzling off. The nightmare continues. I know that if we have to call the drain people and pay them £200, Auntie Ellen will never forgive me. And if she discovers the stain on the carpet she will never forgive Mr Pooter.

At long last, after Holly has come back from the garden, sending filthy looks at Michael, the water level begins to drop. Slowly, slowly, the water drains away. Uncle Mark pulls the chain, and all the kitchen roll is gone. I let out my breath with a sigh of relief. Michael goes, "Yay!" and punches the air.

"Well," says Uncle Mark, "that was an experience."

"Just don't let it happen again," says Auntie Ellen.

"Someone your age… you really ought to have more sense."

"*Kitchen roll*," squeals Holly. "Down the *toilet!*"

Everyone troops back downstairs except me. I go into my bedroom to check on Mr Pooter. He's on the bed, and he's purring. I think that he must be hungry, sicking up all his food, so I get out his tin and show it to him, but he's not interested. I even smear a bit of cat food on my finger in the hope he will lick it off, but he just turns his head away. I think that I will try again later.

I spit on a paper hanky and wipe my finger, then take out my maths book, intending to do some homework. But it's no use, I can't settle. I curl up next to Mr Pooter and press my face into his fur. I tell him that I wish we weren't here. I wish we were somewhere else.

If only we could have stayed with Stevie! Stevie loves Mr Pooter. She loves all cats. She would be able to tell me what to do.

"Let's go down to the garden," I say. I gather Mr Pooter into my arms. It seems safer to carry him; that way, Auntie

Ellen can't complain of cat hairs on her carpet. As we go into the garden, she appears at the back door.

"What were you mopping up, anyway?" she says. "What was it you spilt?"

I don't as a rule tell lies; not if I can help it. But sometimes you just have to. I tell Auntie Ellen that I spilt some water.

"I was carrying Mr Pooter's bowl, and I dropped it."

"Well, just be more careful in future," she says.

Oh, I wish we could be somewhere else!

CHAPTER SIX

Today in the library Mrs Caton gives me a book to read in the holidays. It's called *Three Men in a Boat*, and it's old. I like old books! I like the thought of other people reading them. People from long ago, before I was born. I imagine them turning the pages and chuckling to themselves at bits they find amusing, or maybe going *tut* if there's something they don't approve of, and never dreaming that years later, in another century, someone like me will be turning those same pages and reading the exact same words.

I put the book to my nose and sniff. I always do this with books; Mum used to do it, too. She used to say that the smell of a book was better than the smell of the most expensive perfume. Mrs Caton laughs.

"Why is it that real book people always do that?" she says.

"Do what?" says Jolene, jealously. She likes to think of herself as a book person, in spite of not knowing whether Elinor M. Brent-Dyer goes under B or D. I bet she couldn't get through *Jane Eyre*, even though she is in Year 9. I read it with Mum when I was only ten!

Now I am being boastful. *I have nothing to be boastful about.* Yesterday we had the results of our end-of-term maths exam, and I came next to bottom. On the other hand, I came top of English. Mum would have been ever so proud. She would have said, "You take after me,

Lollipop, you don't have a mathematical brain. You're more of a language person."

But coming next to bottom is nothing to boast about; even Mum would agree with that. So I have absolutely no right to feel superior to Jolene. She might have come *top* of her maths exam, for all I know.

I tell her about books smelling better than perfume, and she does that thing that people are always doing, she looks at me like I'm from outer space.

"Dalek!" she hisses, as she flounces off across the library.

"What did she call you?" says Mrs Caton.

I mutter, "Dalek," hoping that she won't hear and will just forget about it. But she's frowning.

"Why Dalek?" she says.

I say that I don't know.

"It doesn't seem a very pleasant thing to call someone."

I tell her that it's like a sort of nickname. Nickname makes it sound friendly. Mrs Caton doesn't look like she's convinced. She says, "Well, anyway, I was going through my bookshelves and I came across *Three Men in a Boat* and I thought of you immediately. It was written round about the same time as your big favourite, *Diary of a Nobody*. My dad introduced me to it, I used to think it was absolutely hilarious! Mind you, that was when I was about fifteen or sixteen, so I was quite a bit older than you. But you're such a mature reader... I'll be interested to know how you get on. Give it a go, and see what you feel."

I promise her that I will.

"You can read it over the summer holiday. Just a little bit at a time."

Earnestly, I say that I never read books a little bit at a time. "Once I've started I can't stop. I just get greedy and gobble them up!"

"Well, don't get too greedy," says Mrs Caton. "You've got weeks and weeks ahead of you."

The bell rings for the start of afternoon school. Tomorrow is the last day of term. I tell Mrs Caton a big thank you.

"I'll start reading straight away! And I'll take really good care of it."

"I know you will," she says. "You're a book person. But don't forget… a little bit at a time. I don't want you being bored."

I couldn't be bored by a *book*. I tell her this, and she smiles and says, "Different books suit different people… and don't gobble! You've got the whole of the summer."

I go slowly back to class. I can't imagine what I'm going to do all through the summer. I can't imagine not going to the library every day and seeing Mrs Caton. I don't think, really, that I'm looking forward to all those empty weeks.

I used to love the holidays when Mum was here. We never went away anywhere, we couldn't afford it, but we used to go on days out. We used to visit places, all over London. Sometimes out of London, like we'd jump on the train and go to the seaside and buy sticks of rock and paddle and build sandcastles. It was fun! Even if we just packed sandwiches and went to Kensington Gardens to see Peter Pan and feed the ducks. Or like maybe Mum would suddenly say, "Let's go somewhere different! Let's catch a train and just go off… where shall we go to? Tell me which direction! North, east, south, west… you choose!"

So then I'd say, like, "North!" and off we'd go to King's Cross or Euston. We'd look at the indicator boards and Mum would say, "Pick a destination!" I knew I couldn't pick anywhere too far away, like Birmingham or Manchester, but it still gave us lots to choose from.

We didn't really go places so much after Mum was in her wheelchair, but we still had fun. We'd stay home and play games, like Scrabble, or Trivial Pursuit, or Monopoly. We didn't have a Monopoly board, but Mum said that needn't stop us, we'd make one for ourselves. Making the board was almost as much fun as playing the game! We printed out lots of money on the computer and Mum giggled and said, "Let's hope the police don't break in and catch us at it! They'll think we're forgers."

I bet if the police *had* broken in, it would still have been fun. Everything was fun, with Mum. It's not much fun with

Uncle Mark and Auntie Ellen. They never play games, and if I suggested going to the station and choosing a place to visit they'd give me that look, like, *How weird is that child?*

They're going to Wales in August. I suppose I'll go with them, though I don't know where I'll stay. Holly and Michael are staying with their nan, but there isn't room for anyone else so Uncle Mark and Auntie Ellen are booked into a hotel. I don't think Auntie Ellen would want to pay for me to be booked in as well, she's already complaining about how much it costs. So I don't know quite what will happen. Maybe I could go and stay with Stevie, except that Stevie doesn't have people to stay. Perhaps I'll just stay behind, by myself. That would probably be best, otherwise what would happen to Mr Pooter? He couldn't come to Wales, and Auntie Ellen wouldn't pay for a cattery, and anyway he would *hate* being in a cattery. But I'm not leaving him home alone!

When I get back after school I find him curled up on the bed. He chirrups at me, but doesn't get up. I look quickly round to check that he hasn't had any more accidents. Yesterday he was sick on the duvet; just a little bit. I managed to sponge it off. Today I can't see anything. My heart lifts.

"Good boy," I say. "Good boy!" I scratch behind his ears, the way he likes, and try to roll him over to tickle his tummy, but he won't roll. "OK, dinner time," I say. I fetch his bowl and one of his new expensive cat food tins. In the old days he was so eager that he used to jump up and head-butt, and push his way into the bowl before Mum had even had a chance to get the food in there. He doesn't do that, now. I have to coax him.

I take his bowl over to the bed. He doesn't look at it.

"Nice kitty food," I say. "Yum yum!" I pick up the bowl and pretend to eat out of it myself. Mr Pooter watches me, unblinking. "Now you have some!" I offer him the bowl again, but he turns his head away. "Chicken and liver... yummy yummy!" I smear a bit on my finger. His blunt nose crimples. He's almost tempted... and then he turns away again. He's not going to eat, no matter how hard I try.

I sit on the bed, stroking him. Stevie once said that cats are creatures of habit. "They don't like change. Upsets them." I think that maybe Mr Pooter is missing Mum. I whisper, "I miss her, too!" I wish there was something I could do to make him happy. I wish he could creep into my ice house with me. We could huddle there together, and no one could get at us.

I go down to tea, leaving his bowl beside him on the bed. When I come back, it is still there; the food is still in it. I'm beginning to worry. His coat isn't as shiny as it used to be, and I can feel his ribs sticking out. I don't know what to do!

I'm going to ring Stevie; Stevie will know. She knows everything about cats. I take my mobile out of my bag and bring up her number. My heart is thumping. As a rule, in the evening, she doesn't bother to answer. She and Mum had a special code. Mum would let the phone ring three times, then immediately ring again, so that Stevie would know it was her. But I'm not sure she'll remember; her memory isn't what it was. And even if she does, she still mightn't answer. She'll know it can't be Mum.

If she does answer, she'll be cross. She hates people telephoning her. But I have to do it, for Mr Pooter.

I let the phone ring three times and press the off button. Then I ring again, and this time I let it keep ringing. It rings and it rings. I sink down next to Mr Pooter, and for just a minute my ice house begins to crumble. I feel the back of my eyes prickling. And then I hear Stevie's voice, barking into my ear.

"Yes?"

"S-Stevie?" I say.

"Who is this?"

She sounds suspicious. I tell her that it's Laurel. She says, "Laurel Winton? This time of night?"

It's only six o'clock. But Stevie is an old lady. I stammer that I'm really sorry to be a nuisance.

"Well, get on with it," says Stevie. "I'm in the middle of feeding time." And then she shouts, very loudly, "You! Thomas. Get out of that dish!"

I giggle, in spite of myself. She has always had trouble

with Thomas. He's large and stripy and he steals food.

"No laughing matter," grumbles Stevie. "Cat has no morality. What can I do for you?"

I tell her that I'm worried about Mr Pooter. "He doesn't want to eat and he keeps being sick and his ribs are showing!"

"Kidneys," says Stevie.

I swallow. "Is that serious?"

"Old cat. Could be. Needs to go to the vet, get treated."

"Will they be able to make him better?"

Stevie says there are things that can be done. Special diets. Tablets. But I must take him straight away. "No hanging around. Get him there immediately."

I falter. "You mean, like… *now?*"

"Tomorrow. Make an appointment."

I hear myself wailing down the phone, "I don't know where the vet is!"

"Yellow pages," snaps Stevie. "Local library. Ask!" And then, in her gruff, gravelly voice, she goes, "Must look after him. Gave your mum a lot of pleasure. Not fair to let him suffer."

I wouldn't! I wouldn't ever let Mr Pooter suffer. I tell Stevie that I will do what she says. I will find a vet and I will make an appointment.

Talking to Stevie makes me feel strong and confident. I can do what she says. I *will* do what she says. It's for Mr Pooter.

And then I ring off, and bit by bit my confidence starts to trickle away. Instead of feeling strong I feel feeble and useless. I'm not sure that someone of twelve years old *can* make appointments with vets. And even if they can, how am I going to pay? Vets cost money. I don't know how much, but a lot more than my pocket money. What am I going to do?

I look at Mr Pooter, trustfully gazing up at me from the bed, and I know that I have to do *something*. I wish Mum was here! But she isn't. It's up to me. I know what I have to do, I have to get my courage up and ask Uncle Mark.

I go downstairs. Uncle Mark is in his shed. He makes

things in there, bird tables and dolls' houses and stuff, which he sells to people. Mum always said he should have been a carpenter instead of the manager of a DIY shop.

I tell him that Mr Pooter needs to go to the vet. "He's not eating properly. I think it might be his kidneys."

"Well, now, Lol, you have to face it," says Uncle Mark, "he is an old cat. I'm not quite sure how much they can do."

"There's tablets," I say. "They can make him better. *Please!* Can't we make an appointment?"

For a minute I think he's going to say no; but then he sighs and says all right, we'll take him along. "I'll ask next door, they've got a cat. They'll know which the nearest vet is."

I settle down to do my homework, with Mr Pooter sitting next to me. I tell him that we're going to take him to the doctor and get some medicine. I feel happier now that I've talked to Uncle Mark. But then I go downstairs to get a glass of milk and Uncle Mark and Auntie Ellen are in the kitchen and the door is open a crack so that I can hear their voices. I hear Auntie Ellen saying something about "Ridiculous expense" and Uncle Mark saying "All she's got", and I know that they're talking about me and Mr Pooter. I turn, and come rushing back upstairs and into my room, where I fling myself on to the bed and cuddle Mr Pooter as hard as ever I can.

"I love you, I love you, I love you," I whisper, into his fur. Mr Pooter rubs his head against me, and I tell him that everything is going to be all right. I'll look after him.

I decide that I will make a start on *Three Men in a Boat*. It is about these three men who go off in a boat with a dog called Montmorency. I know that it is supposed to be funny because of Mrs Caton telling how me she found it hilarious, so I am trying to find bits that make me laugh. When I find one I am going to write it down in my special notebook that Mum gave me last Christmas. It has a beautiful silk cover, embroidered in bright blues and oranges and emerald greens, with scarlet flowers. I have the page already open, but so far I haven't found anything. It is quite worrying as I am already on page 32. I have to find *something* funny so that I can tell Mrs Caton tomorrow. She would be disappointed if I don't like her book.

There's a bit about Montmorency, saying how his idea of living is to collect a gang of the most disreputable dogs he can find and lead them round town to fight other disreputable dogs. And a bit where J, who is the man telling the story, can't find his coat and grows very cross when none of his friends can find it, either. He says, "You might just as well ask the cat to find anything!" Those bits are quite funny, I suppose. Especially the cat bit. I remember once when Mum had lost the front door key and we were looking all over for it, and Mr Pooter just sat there, with his paws tucked in, watching as we crawled round the room on our hands and knees, peering under the sofa and poking down the sides of chairs. And then he yawned, and stood up, and we discovered that he'd been sitting on it the whole time. Sitting on the front door key! Mum said, "That is just so typical of a cat!"

I am about to take out my pen and start writing things down, to tell Mrs Caton, when Michael knocks at the door and says, "Dad wants you to come downstairs and be with the rest of us." I hesitate. "You're part of the family," says Michael. "You can't keep hiding away."

Reluctantly, I put down my notebook. Michael looks at me. He seems concerned. He says, "Don't you like being with us?"

I feel my cheeks grow pink. I mumble that I don't think Auntie Ellen really wants me here. It's not a criticism! If this was my house, I probably wouldn't want me here.

Now I've made Michael's cheeks go pink, as well. He says that Auntie Ellen is doing her best to make me feel welcome. "She wants you to be happy... I think you should come down."

I leave Mr Pooter curled up on the duvet and obediently go with Michael to join the rest of the family. Holly, very self important, informs me that Auntie Ellen has just finished making her costume for Book Week. "I'm going as a Woodland Fairy...

Holly tree fairy! Can I try it on, Mum?"

She puts it on and starts pirouetting round the room.

"Yuck," says Michael; but he's not being fair. Auntie Ellen is good at sewing. She's made this really brilliant holly costume, all decorated with shiny green leaves and bright red berries.

"Did you ever dress up for Book Week?" says Holly. "What did you dress up as?"

"A pirate," I say.

"A *pirate?* You don't have girl pirates!"

"Why not?" says Michael.

"Cos you don't! Why did you go as a pirate?"

"Just fancied it," I say.

I didn't really fancy it. I really wanted to go as a fairy. Rainbow Fairy. That's what I'd set my heart on. But Mum wasn't ever very good at sewing. My fairy skirt was all limp and saggy, and the top bit didn't fit properly. And when I picked up my fairy wand it immediately collapsed, which made Mum giggle. I didn't giggle; I burst into tears. I sobbed and raged, cos now what was I going to do?

"I look like I'm wearing a dish rag!" I blamed Mum for leaving everything till the last minute. "Like you always do! Everyone else has had their costumes for *weeks*."

Mum immediately stopped giggling and promised that she would make me something else. "Something better! Even if I have to sit up all night." Which she did. She made me this pirate outfit and I wasn't in the least bit grateful. I shouted that I didn't want to be a pirate, I wanted to be a Rainbow Fairy. Poor Mum! She begged me to give her a kiss and say she was forgiven, but I wouldn't. I went off in a sulk and spent the whole day being jealous of all the people who had proper mums, who made them lovely sparkly fairy dresses which didn't sag and bag. I was still cross when I got home. Mum tried so hard to make it up to me.

"Oh, Lollipop, I'm so sorry," she said. "I'm such a rotten mum!"

But she wasn't. She wasn't! She was the best mum anyone ever had. I wish so much that I'd told her so!

I have to go back upstairs. I need to cuddle Mr Pooter.

"Where are you off to?" says Auntie Ellen. "You've only just come down."

I tell her that I have to write a book report for Mrs Caton. "I want to do it while it's fresh in my mind." Auntie Ellen shakes her head, like, *I give up!*

"Go on, then," she says. "If that's what you want."

I gallop back up the stairs. Mr Pooter opens an eye and stretches. I check the room, but I don't think he's moved, so that is all right.

"Good boy," I say. "Good boy!"

I settle down beside him and start writing in my notebook. I put down the bit about Montmorency and his gang of dogs. I put down the cat bit. I can't think of anything else. The truth is, I am finding this book quite difficult to get into. Maybe it is because I am worried about Mr Pooter and not in the right mood. Or maybe it's because this is the first grown-up book that I have tried to read on my own, without Mum. If Mum were reading it to me, and doing all the voices, then I am sure I would find lots to laugh at. But I am not going to give up! I am a real book person and Mrs Caton is eagerly waiting to know how I get on.

On the way in to school this morning Uncle Mark says that he will ring the vet and make an appointment for this evening. Auntie Ellen is with us, as it is one of her days when she works in the shop. She says that she is the one who will be coming with me. My heart goes plummeting. I don't want Auntie Ellen coming with me! But I haven't any choice. It's Thursday, and late-night shopping, and Uncle Mark won't be home in time.

After lunch I go to the library. I take out my notebook and read Mrs Caton the bits I've written down.

"I think those bits were hilarious," I say.

I wasn't quite sure what the word hilarious meant until I looked it up in the dictionary. It means "very funny", and I didn't honestly find either of the bits *very* funny. Just a little bit funny. But Mrs Caton looks pleased.

"I'm so glad you're enjoying it," she says. "I thought you would."

I promise her that I will make a note of all the other bits I find funny, so that I can tell her about them. She says that's a good idea.

"It'll be something to look forward to at the start of next term."

"I'll have finished it long before then," I say. "I'll probably have read a million others by then!"

Now I'm being boastful again. I don't mean to be, but it's probably true, I will have read a million others. There are eight long weeks to go and I can't think what else there'll be to do.

I get home to find Auntie Ellen waiting impatiently for me. "Go and fetch the cat," she says. "Put it in its box, we have to be at the vet for 4.15."

I hate that she calls Mr Pooter "the cat". He's Mr Pooter! I go upstairs to get him and he purrs amiably. I think he quite likes his box. Holly, for some reason, insists on coming with us. She says she's never been to the vet's before and she wants to know what it's like. I tell her it's like being at the doctor's, except all the patients are animals.

We sit in the Reception area, waiting to be called. I hold Mr Pooter on my lap, in his box. He crouches, watchfully. There are other people with cats, some people with dogs, one little girl with a pet rabbit. I try to interest Mr Pooter in the rabbit, but Auntie Ellen tells me sharply not to make a nuisance of myself. All I was doing was just turning his box in the right direction, so he could see! Holly wrinkles her nose and says there's a smell. Auntie Ellen tells her it's disinfectant and she goes, "Ugh! Yuck! Poo!" But then a vet puts his head round the door and calls out, "Fluffy Marshall?" and Holly giggles – "*Fluffy Marshall!*" – and wants to know whether that's the name of the cat or the name of the owner. Auntie Ellen tells her to be quiet and stop showing off, so then she sits in a sulk, scuffing her feet on the floor.

When it's our turn the vet calls, "Pooter Walters!" He's not Pooter Walters, he's Pooter Winton, but I suppose it's not really important. What's important is that the vet is going to make him better.

We all troop into the surgery. The vet asks what the

problem seems to be, and I tell him about Mr Pooter being sick and not wanting to eat.

"And how old is he?" says the vet.

Proudly I say that he's sixteen.

"Quite an old fellow," says the vet.

He examines Mr Pooter all over. Mr Pooter is so good! He doesn't complain once. I stroke him and tell him that everything is going to be all right.

"Well," says the vet, straightening up. "In view of his age, I'd say it's almost certainly a kidney problem, but we'd better do a blood test to make sure."

"Is that really necessary?" says Auntie Ellen.

The vet says if we want a proper diagnosis, it is.

"What I mean," says Auntie Ellen, "is it really worth it? At his age?"

I hold my breath. I squeeze Mr Pooter.

"We can't treat him if we don't know what's wrong," says the vet. "I agree that he's old, but he's not ancient. Cats can easily live to be nineteen or twenty. Even older."

I am so relieved I let out my breath in a big *whoosh*. I

don't think Auntie Ellen is too happy, but she lets the vet take a sample of Mr Pooter's blood. I keep him very close and whisper in his ear and he doesn't even flinch. He is a very brave cat. The vet says the results will be through in a couple of days and then we can decide on the appropriate treatment. In the meanwhile, he says, we should try him with a special diet.

I put Mr Pooter back in his box and we go out to Reception to collect some cans of special cat diet and pay the bill. I am scared when I see how much the bill comes to. I would have to save up my pocket money for months before I would have enough to pay it. Auntie Ellen is outraged. Angrily she drives us home, saying over and over that it is daylight robbery. I tell her that I will pay it back, that Uncle Mark needn't give me any more pocket money until—

"Until kingdom come!" snaps Auntie Ellen. "Don't be absurd."

"It's her cat," says Holly, "so she *ought* to pay it back."

I say that I will. "I promise!"

"It's only fair," says Holly.

Auntie Ellen tell us both to be quiet. "I've had enough for one day."

As soon as we're back I go upstairs with Mr Pooter and ring Stevie. It's only five o'clock, so maybe she won't be too cross. She's not cross at all! She wants to hear about Mr Pooter. I tell her what the vet said and she says that the special diet will help, but if Mr Pooter is still being picky I could try buying some prawns and whizzing them up in the food processor.

"Make them into a nice soft mush… that should tempt him."

I am going to go out first thing tomorrow and buy some prawns with what is left of my pocket money. Before I stop getting pocket money. I am not sure whether Uncle Mark is going to go on giving me any or not. When he came in I told him he needn't, "I'm going to pay back every penny!" Uncle Mark told me not to be silly. He said of course I didn't need to pay him back. But then Holly chimed in with "It's her cat!" and Auntie Ellen said again about daylight robbery. So now I don't really know. That is why I am going to buy the prawns, quickly, while I still can.

CHAPTER SEVEN

Auntie Ellen and Holly are getting ready to go into town to do some shopping. Auntie Ellen wants to know if I'm going with them, but I say I can't as I have to finish reading my book.

"All this reading," says Auntie Ellen, sounding irritable. "There has to be more to life!"

"I just want to finish it," I say.

They're only going to Tesco. I don't know why it makes her so cross, but lots of the things I do make Auntie Ellen cross. I think she doesn't really like me very much. I try to pretend that I don't care. But deep down, I do. I just can't think what to do about it.

As soon as she and Holly are gone, I'm going down to the minimart near the roundabout to buy prawns for Mr Pooter. There! That's it. They've gone. I wait for the sound of Auntie Ellen's car, backing out of the garage, then I snatch up my purse and dash off.

I come back triumphantly with a medium-size bag of frozen prawns. I fetch Mr Pooter from the bedroom so he can see me warm them up under the hot tap and put them in the blender. He sits on the table, looking interested.

"Special treat," I tell him. He's definitely interested. The only time he's ever tasted prawns was one Christmas, when me and Mum had prawn cocktails for a treat and he got so excited he jumped up and started hooking prawns out with his paw. We laughed so much, we didn't have the heart to tell him off. In the end, he ate more prawns than we did. But as Mum said, "It's his Christmas too." I wonder if he remembers?

I put the prawn mush into a plastic pot and carefully wash and dry the blender. I don't want Auntie Ellen knowing what I've done; she'd be sure to disapprove.

"Let's go outside," I say. I pick up the pot, plus Mr Pooter's dish and *Three Men in a Boat*, and Mr Pooter follows me into the garden, where we settle down on the grass and I spoon out some of the mixture. Mr Pooter's nose is twitching. He seems really eager. He's eating! I'm so happy I immediately ring Stevie to tell her. Stevie says that's good. "But only little bits at a time. Don't want him throwing up." I ask her how little the bits should be, and how often I should give them to him, but she just snaps "Common sense!" and rings off. I think perhaps just a couple of blobs every half hour.

I'm working really hard at *Three Men in a Boat*. What I'm doing, I'm imagining that Mum's reading it to me. Every now and again I read bits out loud, pretending that I'm her, and Mr Pooter looks up at me and seems puzzled.

Auntie Ellen and Holly have come back. Auntie Ellen goes into the house with the shopping; Holly comes over to me and Mr Pooter.

"What's that?" she says, pointing to the pot of mashed prawn. I tell her that it's special food for Mr Pooter. She picks it up and sniffs at it.

"Smells like fish… why's it all pink?"

I say that it's pink because it's prawns.

"Prawns for a *cat*?" She shrills it at me, accusingly. Her eyes are popping. "Where'd you get prawns from?"

I tell her that I went down the road and bought them.

"For a *cat*? You could have paid Mum back some of her money!"

"He's not very well," I say. "He needs special food."

"He's a *cat*," says Holly. Her eyes, still popping, swivel round the garden. "I hope he's not doing messes in Mum's flowerbed."

He's just sitting here, minding his own business. Good

as gold, soaking up the sunshine. I cuddle him closer. I feel all the time that I have to protect him. I don't think even Holly would ever do anything mean; it's just that they all seem to hate cats. Except for Michael. He doesn't.

"What are you reading?" says Holly. She peers down at the cover of *Three Men in a Boat*. "Yuck! It's all old men again. What d'you want to keep reading about old men for?"

I say that I don't *specially* want to read about old men.

"So why do it?" she says.

I tell her because someone lent it to me. "A friend."

"What friend?" Holly pops her eyes at me. "You haven't got any friends."

I have, too! I say, "Mrs Caton, if you must know."

Holly demands to know who Mrs Caton is. I tell her that she's our school librarian.

"And she's your *friend*? She can't be your friend. She's like a teacher! Teachers can't be your friend."

Mrs Caton *is* my friend. She wouldn't have lent me *Three Men in a Boat* if she wasn't.

Holly stands, frowning. I try to go on reading, but I can't with her standing there. I wish she'd go away!

"You know those shorts you've got on?" she says. "They're really gross!"

I feel my cheeks start to fire up. I know my shorts are old and a bit washed-out. They weren't even a very good colour to start with; a sort of egg yolk yellow. I got them last year at the Oxfam shop. But it's rude of Holly to say they're gross!

"Mum was going to take you into town tomorrow," she says. "She was going to get you some new stuff for when we go on holiday. But I don't know whether she will, now. Not after having to pay all that money to the vet. She isn't *made* of money."

I say that's all right, I don't want new clothes.

"Well, you can't go away looking like that," says Holly.

So maybe I'll stay behind. I will stay behind! I'm not leaving Mr Pooter. He needs me to look after him.

There's a long silence. I read the same sentence three times without taking it in. Holly tosses her head.

"Well, if you don't want to talk," she says.

She goes off in a huff. I feel that I may have been ungracious, but I don't think, really, that she was trying to be friendly.

I feed Mr Pooter another blob of prawn and read a bit more of *Three Men in a Boat*. It's hot in the sunshine and I'm finding it quite difficult to concentrate. But I am definitely going to finish this book! Mrs Caton will be so disappointed if I don't.

Auntie Ellen has come into the garden. She says that tomorrow she is taking me into town to go clothes shopping. I tell her – very politely – that she really doesn't have to.

"Unfortunately, I do," says Auntie Ellen. "I can't have you going round like some waif that's got all its clothes from an Oxfam shop."

Does she know that this is where me and Mum used to buy most of our stuff? You can find good bargains! It's true, however, that you do sometimes have to put up with egg yolk yellow cos it's all they have in your size. I say to

Auntie Ellen that it honestly doesn't bother me, clothes aren't that important, though even as I'm saying it I can't help thinking that it would be nice, just for once, to be able to go into a proper shop and choose.

Auntie Ellen says that it may not bother *me*, but it bothers her. "I'm not having people say that I'm not doing my duty by you!"

At tea time the telephone rings and Uncle Mark goes to answer it. When he comes back he says it was the vet.

"They've had the results of the blood test. You can go in tomorrow to pick up some tablets."

"And how much are they going to cost?" says Auntie Ellen.

Uncle Mark says he doesn't know. "But if he has to have them—"

"Well, does he?" says Auntie Ellen. "That's the question, isn't it?"

Her eyes bore into Uncle Mark. Uncle Mark seems uncomfortable. He clears his throat and pours himself another cup of tea. I glance anxiously from him to Auntie

Ellen and back again. Why doesn't Uncle Mark say something?

"They can't be that much," he mumbles. "They're just giving us a fortnight's supply to start with. See how he gets on."

Auntie Ellen purses her lips. "And what happens then?"

"Then they..." Uncle Mark waves a hand. "Review the situation."

"And so do we," says Auntie Ellen.

What does she mean? What is she talking about?

"Pity they don't have a national health service for animals," says Michael.

"They do," says Auntie Ellen. "It's called insurance. Responsible pet owners *insure* their animals."

"Yes, well, Sue probably couldn't afford it," says Uncle Mark.

Auntie Ellen's lips go all pinched and narrow. "If you can't afford them, you shouldn't have them. It's the same with children. Holly, stop messing your food around! Laurel, get on and eat."

I dredge up a forkful of spaghetti and suck it into my mouth. I have to force myself to swallow it; it's like worms slithering down my throat. I'm just not hungry. I push my plate away and ask to be excused.

"I really don't know why I bother," says Auntie Ellen.

Next morning, on the way into town, we stop off at the vet to collect Mr Pooter's tablets. The nurse starts to explain to Auntie Ellen how he has to have two a day, one in the morning and one in the evening, but Auntie Ellen stops her.

"It's my niece's cat. She's the one who needs to know."

Auntie Ellen goes off to pay the bill. She comes back looking grim. We pile into the car and Holly whines that we're going the wrong way.

"We're going back home," says Auntie Ellen.

"But you said we were going into town! You said you were going to buy her some new clothes! You s— "

"I know what I said." Auntie Ellen pulls up at some traffic lights. She does it so viciously the car almost stands on its head. "The clothes will have to wait."

"But she can't go away like that!" Holly bounces round in the front seat to look at me. I'm wearing the shorts again, and an old T-shirt. "What'll Nan say?"

I clutch Mr Pooter's tablets. I don't care about the shorts! I just want Mr Pooter to get well.

Auntie Ellen says it can't be helped. "Beggars can't be choosers." She says she is going to go through my wardrobe and see what I have that is wearable.

As soon as we get back I go upstairs to give Mr Pooter his first tablet. He won't take it! He won't open his mouth and I don't know what to do. I ring Stevie and wail at her. She says, "Oh, for goodness' sake!" She is always very impatient with anyone who doesn't know as much about cats as she does. She wasn't with Mum, but that was because Mum was special.

"I've tried and tried," I whimper.

For a moment I think she's just going to bark "Common sense!" and ring off, but instead she heaves this big disgruntled sigh, like *how can anyone be that useless*, and says, "Grab his ruff, back of neck. Soon as his mouth opens, pop tablet in, close mouth, rub throat. Make sure he swallows. Nothing to it."

I say a humble thank you and turn sternly to Mr Pooter, who's watching me from the bed.

"I don't want any more trouble," I say. "You have to take your medicine."

I'm a bit nervous, cos I don't want to hurt him. Very gently, I do what Stevie says. His mouth opens, so I can see all the pretty pink ridges. In goes the tablet. I rub his throat, and he swallows. It works, it works! I almost ring Stevie back to tell her, but think perhaps I'd better not.

I spend the morning in my room, reading *Three Men in a Boat*. We can't go down to the garden because two of Holly's friends have come by and they're all out there, shrieking and running about. Holly wouldn't like it if they saw me in my gross egg yolk shorts. I could put something else on, but probably she wouldn't like it whatever I wore. Anyway, Mr Pooter might be frightened; he's not used to people running about.

After lunch, Auntie Ellen takes Holly to the dentist, so me and Mr Pooter sit outside where I finish Mrs Caton's book. I decide to write a review of it, specially for Mrs Caton. This is some of what I write,

THREE MEN IN A BOAT by Jerome K. Jerome

This book was written in 1889. It is about three men and their dog who all go off together in a boat. In places it is quite amusing. For instance,

And then I have copied bits from the book, to show that I have read it properly and not just skipped.

I come back upstairs with Mr Pooter and write it out again, nicely, in my best handwriting. Then I do a title page:

REVIEW OF THREE MEN IN A BOAT
by Laurel Winton

and draw a picture of the three men and their dog. I don't draw the boat, as I can only do people, but I think Mrs Caton will be pleased with it. I wish I could give it to her straight away! I want her to know how quickly I have managed to get through the book. I'm sure it will surprise her.

I wonder where she lives and whether she is in the telephone directory. If it is somewhere not too far away I could go and visit her. I could take her book back, and I could – I could lend her *Diary of a Nobody*! She would like that. I felt really honoured when she lent me *Three Men in a Boat*, cos you don't lend books to just anyone. You only lend them to people you can trust, not to people who are going to lose them or forget to give them back. If I lend Mrs Caton my copy of *Diary of a Nobody* she will know that I trust her.

I go downstairs and find the local directory. I don't know whether Caton is a common name or not. Catley, Catlin, Catmull... Caton! There is only one in there. Caton, C. Mrs Caton's first name is Christine. It must be her! I write down the address, 28 Denning Avenue, Horley Wood. I don't know where Horley Wood is, but there is a street map by the telephone. I look up Denning Avenue, and it doesn't seem like it's too far, except I don't know how to get there.

Michael is in the front room, doing things on the computer. I ask him if he knows where Horley Wood is. He says yes, why? I tell him that I want to go there.

"To Horley Wood?" He sounds surprised. "There's nothing there."

I say that I know someone. "A friend."

He looks at me, oddly. He doesn't actually say "But you don't have any friends!" Still, I know that that is what he is thinking.

"Can I walk there?" I say. Michael says no, I'd have to get a bus, but he doesn't know which one.

"D'you want me to find out?" He goes to Google and puts in Horley Wood. "There you are… 129 goes all the way. You can pick it up down the road."

I'm so grateful that I say thank you about a million times. Michael looks embarrassed and says, "You're welcome." And then he says, "So when are you going? Not right now?"

I say no, tomorrow.

"Mum could probably drive you there," says Michael, "if you wanted. It'd only take about ten minutes."

I tell him that I'd rather get the bus. "I don't like having to ask Auntie Ellen for things."

There's a bit of a pause, then Michael says, "OK."

I think he understands.

CHAPTER EIGHT

I wake up feeling happy. Mr Pooter is eating his special cat food and has stopped being sick, and I am going to see Mrs Caton! I am quite excited. She will be so pleased that I liked her book.

I put *Three Men in a Boat* and *Diary of a Nobody* in my bag. It occurs to me that really I ought to telephone first, to check that Mrs Caton will be there, but I am not very good on the telephone. And anyway, I want it to be a surprise!

I tell Auntie Ellen that I am going to visit someone.

"Who's that?" she says. "Someone from school?"

"It's that woman!" shrieks Holly. "I bet it's that woman!"

Auntie Ellen immediately wants to know which woman.

"That woman that's a teacher," says Holly.

I say she's not a teacher, she's a librarian.

"Mrs Caton?" says Michael. "You're going to see Mrs Caton?"

"Has she invited you?" says Auntie Ellen.

Before I can answer, Holly's chipped in with, "She thinks she's her friend!"

I say, "She is my friend. I'm taking her book back to her."

"Well, don't outstay your welcome," says Auntie Ellen. "Where does she live? Do you need a lift?"

Michael nods at me, but I tell Auntie Ellen that I can catch the bus. I add that I'm quite used to finding my way around.

"Very well," says Auntie Ellen. "But take your phone, just in case. Give me a ring if you need picking up. Do you have enough for your bus fare?"

Oh! My face falls; I hadn't thought of bus fares. I used up most of my pocket money on prawns and special cat food tins. Auntie Ellen, as if resigned, takes out her purse and gives me some pound coins. Holly sends me this really *filthy* look.

"You're mad," says Michael, following me out of the room. "Mum could have got you there in ten minutes... she did offer!"

How can I explain that I want to go by myself? It would ruin things if Auntie Ellen took me. It would make it feel sort of... *tainted*. But I can't say this to Michael.

"Is Mrs Caton really your friend?" he says.

I tell him yes. "We're both book people."

I can see he thinks it a bit odd, but he says he's glad I've found someone. "It must have been hard, starting a new school in the middle of term. And some of those girls, they can be really mean."

I've already forgotten about them; they don't bother me. Nothing bothers me, now that Mr Pooter's getting better.

"Well, have a nice day," says Michael.

He is such a polite boy. I really like him.

It takes me ages to walk to the bus stop, and then I have to wait fifteen minutes for the bus, but I don't mind. I'm fizzing with anticipation. I imagine Mrs Caton's face when she sees me on the doorstep.

"What? You've read it so soon?" she goes. (In my imagination, that is.) She invites me in so that she can read my review. We have this long, cosy chat together, all about books, and I lend her *Diary of a Nobody*. She promises she will read it straight away. "I'll call and let you know," she goes (still in my imagination). "Then you can come round again and we can read *my* review!"

She might even lend me something else.

Of course, she may not be there; I have to be prepared for that. But I've brought a pen with me, and some paper, and I can always write her a note. Then she can ring me and I can come back another day.

I find her road quite easily. It is a tiny close and her house is the second one along. I ring the bell and wait, anxiously. I really hope she's in!

The door opens. Two small children are standing there; a girl and a boy. I never thought of Mrs Caton having children. The little boy has jam all over his face; the girl is covered in what looks like flour. Solemnly she says, "This is the Caton residence."

I ask her if Mrs Caton is in. She turns and shouts, "Mu-u-um!" and Mrs Caton appears. She is carrying a mixing bowl and beating something with a wooden spoon.

"Laurel!" she says. "What on earth are you doing here?"

She sounds every bit as surprised as I thought she

would; just not in the way that I imagined. Suddenly, I'm feeling a bit uncertain.

"Why are you here?" she says.

I swallow, and say that I've brought her book back.

"You didn't have to do that," she says. "I told you, next term. How did you find my address?"

Something isn't right. She doesn't seem happy to see me. I mumble that I looked her up in the telephone directory.

"Well, you really shouldn't have come here, you know." She hands the mixing bowl to the little girl and tells her to take it back to the kitchen. "It isn't right."

I swallow, and hold out the book. She takes it from me. She doesn't even ask me if I enjoyed it.

"I… I've… done a review." I pull it out of my bag. She looks at it, frowning. "And I've brought you *Diary of a Nobody!*"

"Laurel, I'd honestly rather not," she says. "Not right now. Bring it next term, will you? Will you do that?"

I nod, miserably.

"Please don't be upset," says Mrs Caton. "I'm sure you meant well, but you must see, it's not really appropriate. You can't just call round like this. Apart from anything else—" She smiles at me, trying to make a joke of it. "It's holiday time! Even librarians need a break."

I stammer that I thought we were friends.

"Well, of course we're friends! *School* friends." She takes the review from me, but not *Diary of a Nobody*. "Next term we'll have a good long talk about *Three Men in a Boat*. Meanwhile, I'll look forward to reading what you have to say about it. All right?" She smiles again, and I do my best to smile back. "That's better! Now, you'll have to excuse me, we're in the middle of baking a cake. It's Sally's birthday tomorrow and she's having a party, so it's all a bit hectic, I'm afraid. See you in September!"

I turn, and trail down the path. I shouldn't have come. I have been *intrusive*. Mrs Caton isn't really my friend; she was just pretending, because she feels sorry for me. And now I've made a nuisance of myself, trying to force *Diary of a Nobody* on her. She obviously doesn't want to read it. She was just trying to keep me happy. I feel so humiliated.

Slowly, I retrace my steps to the bus stop. I desperately, desperately don't want to go back. If it wasn't for Mr Pooter, I might even run away. Except what would I do? Where would I go?

A bus comes along and I get on it. Half an hour later I'm walking up the path, using my key to let myself in. I can't see any sign of Holly or Michael, but I can hear Auntie Ellen on the phone. I start up the stairs, and there is Holly, waiting for me on the landing.

"You're back," she says. She pushes past and goes galloping down, yelling, "Mum, she's back!"

I go into my bedroom – and my heart almost stops beating. The rug which I used to cover up Mr Pooter's sick has been removed, and there on the pink carpet, just inside the door, is an ugly yellow stain.

I hear Auntie Ellen's voice, calling up the stairs,

"Laurel! Can you come down here, please?"

My heart starts up again, *bam bam bam*, thudding and panicking inside my rib cage. Auntie Ellen is waiting for me, at the end of the hall.

"Come out here," she says. "I want a word with you." She is looking very grim. We go into the kitchen and firmly she closes the door on Holly. "Sit down." She points to a chair. I sit, stiffly, on the edge of it. "Right! Now, what do you have to say for yourself?"

I don't ask, *about what?* I am not brave enough; and anyway, I know.

"I asked you a question," says Auntie Ellen. "I should like an answer."

I open my mouth, but nothing comes out. I'm not making any sound. I can't speak!

"All right." Auntie Ellen pulls out a chair and sits down opposite me. "Let's try it another way… what is that stain on your bedroom carpet?"

I sit, silent and frozen. Auntie Ellen drums her fingers.

"Laurel! I'm waiting. Will you please tell me… *what is that stain?*"

"It's… "

"It's what? It's cat sick, isn't it?"

I nod, miserably.

"And you put the rug over it in the hope I wouldn't notice!" Her voice has gone all Welsh and sing-song, swooping up and down. I shrink back on to my chair. "If you'd owned up at the time," says Auntie Ellen, "we might have been able to do something about it. It's far too late, now. It'll never come out. The carpet's ruined."

I manage to croak that I'm sorry.

"Sorry?" The word comes out as a hiss. I see a little spray of spit fly through the air. "Sorry's not good enough! I know you were brought up to believe it didn't matter if you lived in a pigsty, but we happen to have higher standards. We like the place to look decent. That's my mother's room, you know… the room she stays in when she's here. We only did it up last year, we got that carpet new. Now what am I to do? You think we're made of money?"

I shake my head and say again that I'm sorry.

"It's not much use being sorry after the event. Why didn't you tell me at the time?"

I whisper that I was too scared.

"Scared? What do you have to be scared of? Has anyone ever lifted a finger against you?"

"I was scared—" I gulp down a lump that's blocking my throat— "that you'd blame Mr Pooter."

"I don't blame dumb animals," says Auntie Ellen. "I blame the owners. For goodness' sake, Laurel! You're old enough to know better."

I suddenly jump up. "I'll go and scrub it!"

"Scrubbing won't do any good, it's soaked in. The carpet's ruined, just accept it. But if that cat is going to keep being sick all over the place—"

"He's not!" The words come wailing out of me. "He's getting better, he's not doing it any more!"

"Cats shouldn't be in bedrooms anyway," says Auntie Ellen. "They should be outside."

"Oh, please," I say, "please! He can't stay outside, he's old, he's not used to it! He might get attacked, he might get lost, he'd be so confused… *please* don't say he has to go outside!"

Auntie Ellen stands up and begins clattering saucepans in the sink. "I don't know," she says. "I shall have to think about it."

"*Please*," I beg.

"Laurel, I know things have been difficult for you," says Auntie Ellen, "but you have to understand that they've been difficult for us, as well. It's very disruptive, having to take someone in. We were quite prepared to do it, after all you're family, but you really haven't made things easy. You block the toilet, you cost us a small fortune in vet's fees, and now you've ruined a perfectly good carpet. What do you want me to say? Just go on and ruin the rest of the room? Ruin the rug, ruin the duvet? It may be the way you were used to living, but it's not the way we live here!"

I hang my head and stare down, fixedly, at my feet.

They seem an extraordinarily long way away. It's like they're in a mist. I can't see them properly, my eyes are all wet.

Why? Why are they wet? I draw myself up. I am an ice lolly. Frozen solid. Back, back, into my ice house! I breathe, deeply, and the wetness turns to frost.

"Laurel?"

I jerk my head up.

"Are you listening?"

I say yes; I'm listening.

"If it happens one more time—"

What? I look straight into her eyes, daring her to say it. Say it, say it! She drops her gaze.

"Just make sure that it doesn't," she says.

Out in the hall I find Holly; I suppose she's been listening. She calls after me as I go back upstairs, "I don't know what's going to happen when my nan comes to stay!"

They all go out in the afternoon. I sit in the garden with Mr Pooter and think about running away. There's only one place I could go, and that is back to London. To Stevie. What would she say if I turned up on the doorstep? She would be even less pleased than Mrs Caton. But I don't think she would turn me away. She certainly wouldn't turn Mr Pooter away. Stevie would do anything for a cat.

I haven't any money, and I don't know for certain that Uncle Mark is going to give me any. Not now that Auntie Ellen has discovered the carpet. He might say I can't have any more until I've paid for a new one.

But that is all right. There is a pot in the kitchen cabinet where Auntie Ellen puts all her loose change; everything from 20p down to 1p. Mum and me used to have a pot like that. When it was full we used to give it to Stevie for her cat charity. Auntie Ellen uses hers to buy treats. I know it would be stealing if I took it, but I don't really care. I *would* care, if it was for cats. Or any other charity, if it comes to that. But it isn't, so I don't.

By the end of the afternoon I have taken the money and put Mr Pooter in his carrying box and caught the bus into town. I've gone to the station and bought a ticket for London and am on my way to Stevie's. In my imagination, that is. I haven't quite got around to imagining what Stevie will say, but that is not important. Whatever she says, I know she will look after Mr Pooter. That is all that matters.

I feel strong now that I have worked out a plan. Even when the car arrives back and Holly comes into the garden and starts on again about the carpet, it's like she is just a fly buzzing against a window pane.

"Don't you have anything to say?" she says.

No. I have nothing to say.

"You'd think you'd at least be *sorry*."

I rub my cheek against Mr Pooter's fur.

"Mum loved that carpet," says Holly. "She chose it specially... it's dusky pink."

I think, hysterically, that now it's sickly yellow; and without warning a mad giggle bursts out of me.

"You're *evil*," says Holly. "You know that? You're evil!"

She runs off, into the house. I think that I probably

ought to be upset – or insulted – or something. But I'm not. I'm not anything. I'm inside my ice house, clutching Mr Pooter, and there isn't anything anyone can say or do that will get to me.

Later on, I'm in my room. Uncle Mark is back from work and we have had tea, and now I have come up here to be with Mr Pooter. I know Auntie Ellen hates him being downstairs, but I won't leave him on his own. He likes to be with people. Mum said that when I was at school he used to sit on her lap all day long. Even though she couldn't get out, she never felt lonely with Mr Pooter to keep her company. He's the most loyal cat there ever was! He never left Mum's side, and now that he's old I won't leave his.

There is a tap at the door and Michael's voice asks if he can come in. I am glad it is Michael and not Holly. He comes over to the bed, where I am sitting with Mr Pooter.

"How is he?" he says.

I say that he is much better now that he is taking his tablets. "He's eating properly – and he's not being sick any more!"

I say this in case Auntie Ellen has sent him up here to spy, though I don't think that is why he has come. He seems to want to say something, but doesn't quite know how. He's standing there, looking awkward.

"What're you reading?" he says.

I show him.

"*Little Women?*" He pulls a face. "Isn't that a bit yucky?"

I tell him that it was one of Mum's favourites, and mine, too.

"Don't you ever read ordinary books?" he says.

I frown and ask him what he means by "ordinary books".

He says, "I dunno... the sort of stuff that girls usually read. Stuff that Holly reads."

I tell him, not meaning to brag or anything, that I have grown out of the sort of stuff that Holly reads, but

I do read lots of teenage books. "It's just that I haven't actually got any."

I used to get them from the library. I went to the library practically every week. Sometimes, as well as books for me, I'd pick up ones that Mum had ordered, then I'd stagger back triumphantly with my school bag full to bursting. I can't go to the library now cos there isn't one. Not anywhere close.

"I can always go up the attic for you," says Michael. "Get you something down." He reaches out a hand and strokes Mr Pooter's head. There's a silence. He's definitely trying to say something, but I don't know what. And then, abruptly, he says it, "I just heard Mum and Dad talking. I heard Mum saying that it's time—" He stops. Little by little, I start to edge back into my ice house. Michael swallows. "She said, *it's time that cat went.* She said she can't have the place ruined and they can't afford to keep paying out small fortunes to the vet."

There is another silence; longer, this time. I curl myself up, a tight ball in the middle of the ice.

"Dad said… he said he couldn't do it to you. Then Mum said, *But you don't mind doing it to me.*"

"Doing what?" I say. My voice is quite calm and steady. Just a bit frosted, because of the ice.

"Well, like… letting the place be messed up and everything?" I see Michael's eyes flicker across to the yellow stain on the carpet. "I didn't hear any more cos they stopped talking soon as they realised I was there. So I don't know if Mum – if she managed to – to talk Dad round. She usually does. But maybe this time… I don't know. I just thought I ought to – well, like, warn you. Or something. Cos I know how you love Mr Pooter!"

He is so embarrassed, he is practically squirming. I felt like telling him, *it's all right, I'm in my ice house.*

Desperately he says, "Maybe you could talk to Dad. He's on your side, he really is! It's just that Mum… she kind of bullies him. You know?"

I nod.

"So you'll talk to him, yeah?"

I say maybe.

"I think you should," says Michael. "Cos otherwise—"

Otherwise, Auntie Ellen will have her way. But even if she doesn't – even if Uncle Mark sticks up for me – I would still be scared to go out and leave Mr Pooter alone with her. I would be scared of coming back and finding him not there. So I am not going to talk to Uncle Mark. I know what I am going to do.

I call after Michael, as he leaves the room. "Is it tomorrow you're going to visit your auntie?"

"Auntie Mei. Yes! We're all going," says Michael. "You're coming with us."

"I think p'raps I'll stay behind," I say.

"You can't do that," he says. "We're going to be out all day! Mum won't let you."

She can't *make* me go.

CHAPTER NINE

"Well, it's her choice," says Auntie Ellen. "If she prefers to shut herself away—"

"No, no, we can't have that!" says Uncle Mark. "She's family, of course she must come. She's been invited."

"For heaven's sake, if the child doesn't *want* to," says Auntie Ellen. She sounds exasperated. "Why force her?"

"Yes," says Holly. "Why force her?"

"No one's forcing her," says Uncle Mark. "I'd just feel happier if she came."

They argue for a while, then Auntie Ellen says, "Laurel, just make up your mind! Are you coming, or not?"

Uncle Mark looks at me almost pleadingly. "Laurel?" he says. I stay silent, trying to do it in an apologetic kind of way, as I would hate for Uncle Mark's feelings to be hurt.

"Oh, for goodness' sake!" snaps Auntie Ellen. "Just leave her. She's old enough to know her own mind."

Auntie Ellen wins, like she always does. For once I'm relieved, though I do feel a bit sorry for Uncle Mark, especially when he asks me if I'm sure I'll be all right, left on my own.

"We're not likely to get back till some time this evening. It's going to be a long day."

I tell him that I don't mind being on my own, and he goes off shaking his head and looking worried, which makes me feel guilty. Uncle Mark has been kind to me. He's tried his best and I know he loved Mum in spite of them being so different. He is always talking about his "little sis". But I have to look after Mr Pooter!

I watch from my bedroom window as the car pulls out of the drive. As soon as it has gone, I take Mr Pooter's carrying box from the bottom of the wardrobe and settle him in it, with one of my sweaters for him to lie on. Then I pack my school bag with as many clothes as I can cram in, and sit down to write a note for Uncle Mark. I have been composing it in my head all night and know exactly what I'm going to say.

Dear Uncle Mark,

Please don't be upset but I am running away with Mr Pooter to keep him safe as I know Auntie Ellen does not like him in her house.

Thank you very much for all that you have done for me, and especially for paying the vet's bills. I know they were expensive.

Yours sincerely, Laurel

PS I am very sorry that I have had to use some of the money from Auntie Ellen's pot but I needed it for my train fare. I promise I will do my best to pay it back.

I take one last look round the room and realise that I can't possibly go without *Diary of a Nobody*. I squash it in amongst my clothes. Then I see Blue Bunny, forlornly sitting on my pillow, so I squash him in as well. I hate leaving all the rest of Mum's books behind, especially as I am not sure Auntie Ellen will ever let me have them back, but what else can I do? I know that Mum will understand. She loved her books, but she loved Mr Pooter more.

I pick him up in his carrying box, sling my bag over my shoulder, and go downstairs into the empty house. I think the best place to leave my note would probably be on the kitchen table. I put an apple on top of it, to keep it from blowing away. Auntie Ellen's pot of money is in the kitchen cabinet. I tip it out on to the table and begin to separate all the 10 and 20p pieces. I feel like a criminal. I hope, if Mum is watching, she understands why I am doing it. Silently I explain to her that it's not for me, it's for Mr Pooter. And I *will* pay it back, just as soon as I'm old enough to start earning money.

There is too much to go in my purse, so I have to use a plastic food bag, which I bury under all the knickers and T-shirts I'm taking with me. It is very heavy, and so is Mr Pooter in his carrying box. It takes me for ever to reach the bus stop as I have to keep breaking off to give my arms a rest. But I get there in the end and sit on the seat in the sunshine, waiting for the bus. I keep talking to Mr Pooter and telling him that we are going to Stevie's. He loves Stevie! All cats love her. She is truly a cat person.

At last we reach the station. It is a good thing the bus stops practically outside as I am not sure how much further I could walk, carrying Mr Pooter. Well, I would have to, of course; if it was a mile I would still walk it. But I am very glad that it is not.

I buy a single ticket to London from one of the machines and go to look at the indicator board to check the next train and see which platform it leaves from. Mum would be proud of me, finding my way round! I am rather proud of me myself. I am sure Holly couldn't do it, she is too used to being taken everywhere by car. I know she is only ten, but I think even when I was ten I would have had no problem.

Once we are on the train, I start to relax. I wonder whether I should call Stevie and tell her we are coming, but I am not quite brave enough. She always sounds so angry over the telephone. And she is sure to be in, because she always is. She never leaves her cats, except just to go shopping.

It takes fifty minutes to reach London. I remember, from when me and Mum came by train. I was younger, then, and it seemed like a really long journey. Now it seems quite short, it seems like we are rushing to our destination at the speed of light. I think this is perhaps because I am a little bit anxious about what is going to happen when we get there. Partly I am anxious about Stevie and what she will say. I know she will welcome Mr Pooter, but I am not so sure she will welcome me. She really hates having people in her house! The other thing which makes me apprehensive is the journey from King's Cross to Gospel Road. I *think* I can remember how it is done, and even if I can't I can always find out. But how will I manage, on tubes and buses, with Mr Pooter? Well, I will just have to, that is all.

Quite suddenly, from somewhere inside my bag, my phone starts up. It startles me. Who can it be? Who has my number? Only Stevie! And, of course, Uncle Mark… I scrabble to get it out before it stops ringing.

Guardedly, I say, "Hello?"

I don't recognise the voice at the other end. It's a woman's voice, very light and clear. "Is that Laurel?" it says. "Laurel, this is Andrea Stafford. I don't know whether your mum ever mentioned me?"

I say no, she didn't, hoping that it doesn't sound rude. The name seems sort of familiar, though I can't think why. I'm sure I never heard it from Mum.

I listen in bewilderment as this unknown person tells me how she and Mum used to be best friends when they were at uni. Why is she ringing me and where did she get my number?

"Your mum wrote me a letter," she says. "Oh, ages ago! Months ago. But she sent it via my publishers and I'm afraid they've only just forwarded it to me. I just got it yesterday."

Now I remember. The letter I faithfully promised Mum that I would put in the post, and never did. Not until it was too late. I ought to confess, but I don't really know who this person is. She might be cross.

"Laurel," she says, "I was devastated when I heard what had happened. Your mum and I were so close! Even though we lost touch, I have never, ever stopped thinking of her. As soon as I got the letter I tried telephoning, but there wasn't any reply, so I rushed straight up here this morning, to your old address. That was when I discovered. Your neighbour – Miss Murray?

She gave me the number of your mobile. In fact I'm here with her right now, I don't know if you'd like to sp—"

And then the phone goes dead. No signal. I switch it off and sit staring. I still can't quite make out who this woman is. *Andrea.* Mum never talked of anyone called Andrea. And imagine Stevie letting her into her house! Stevie never lets people into her house. She'll be cross as hornets. I start to tremble and wonder what I am going to do if Stevie won't let me stay. I can't go back to Uncle Mark's! Not now I've stolen Auntie Ellen's money.

The phone rings again and cautiously I switch it on.

"Laurel?" It's her again. Andrea. "Sorry, something happened. You cut out."

"I'm on a train," I say. "We went through a tunnel."

"Oh! You're travelling? This obviously isn't a good time. Should I call you back later?"

I shake my head. "No, it's all right. I'm... I'm on my way to Stevie!" I forget that she probably doesn't know who Stevie is. "Could you tell her I've got Mr Pooter?"

"Mr Pooter?" She sounds surprised, but in a joyful kind of way. "He's still with you? He must be such an old boy! Oh, I would so love to see him again!"

"Please can you tell Stevie?" I say.

"Stevie?" she says. "You mean Miss Murray? You're bringing him here, to Miss Murray?"

"Yes!" I almost shout it down the telephone. "I'm rescuing him!"

There is a slight pause. I hear the muffled sound of voices. Then she says, "Laurel, where are you, exactly?"

I look out of the window and see the words **KING'S CROSS** slide by.

"Coming into the station," I say.

"Which station?"

"King's Cross."

"And you've actually got Mr Pooter with you? In a basket?"

"In his box. Stevie gave it to me."

"Right. OK! Now, look, here's what we'd like you to do… we'd like you to jump in a cab and come straight here. Can you do that? If you can't, just stay put and I'll come and get you."

I try not to be insulted at her thinking I might not be capable of finding a cab. She's not to know I used to find them for Mum all the time. But I don't have any money left! I tell Andrea this and she says not to worry. "I'll pay for the cab. Just get yourself here."

The train pulls in, and we stand waiting for the doors to open. I remember last time I was with Mum, when she couldn't walk too well, how a kind man helped her off; how we made our way together, very slowly, across the station to the cab rank. Now I'm on my own, just me and Mr Pooter. It is a comfort to think that Mum's friend is waiting for me at Stevie's. I think it might be a bit scary, otherwise.

As soon as I am in the cab, I call Stevie's number.

"Laurel Winton," barks Stevie, "is that you? What on earth do you think you're playing at?"

I tell her that I had to come. "They were going to get rid of Mr Pooter!"

Stevie just grunts. Then Andrea comes on the phone. "Laurel, did you get a cab all right? Good girl! We'll expect you in about twenty minutes."

I try not to watch the meter ticking up as we sit in traffic. It was late in the evening when me and Mum travelled back in a taxi, and the streets were almost empty. Even then Mum joked that we would have to live on bread and water for a week. I wonder if Andrea knows how much it is going to cost, or whether she will be horrified, like Auntie Ellen was when she saw the vet's bill. Maybe, I think to myself hopefully, she is rich and it won't bother her.

As we turn into Gospel Road I feel a shiver run through me. I feel that I should be excited, as if I'm coming home; but Mum isn't there, and it's not my home any more. Someone who must be Andrea is waiting outside Stevie's. She is tall and slim, with sleek black hair and piercing blue eyes. I feel that she is familiar, but I can't think why. The minute she sees the taxi, she comes running to meet us.

"You got here! Thank goodness, I've been so worried. Oh, and there's Mr Pooter! Just as I remember him… I'm Andi, by the way. Let me pay the cab, and we'll go inside and talk."

Andi. That's the name inside Mum's *Diary of a Nobody.*

"Let me have Mr Pooter!" She takes the carrying box from me. "How ever did you manage? He's really heavy!"

Stevie is waiting at the front door. She looks cross. "All this coming and going! All this telephoning! Constant disruption. Well, come along, come along, don't just stand there, letting my cats out. Get inside!"

I scuttle through the door, followed by Andi.

"What is all this nonsense?" demands Stevie, taking Mr Pooter out of his box. "Who's trying to get rid of him?"

"Auntie Ellen," I say. " She doesn't like him! He was

sick on her carpet and now she doesn't want him in the house any more. She says animals shouldn't be in the house. She says it's time he went, she's not going to pay any more vet's bills, it's just a waste of money and—"

"And what? She's going to get him put down? Over my dead body!" Stevie stumps off towards the kitchen, Mr Pooter in her arms. A gaggle of cats trail after her. "You two—" Stevie waves a hand, "in there and do your talking. Get things sorted. I don't want to hear from you till you've done."

Meekly, me and Andrea go into the front room. Cats stare at us from the sofa, from chairs, from the table. Andrea wrinkles her nose, and I do the same. We look at each other and pull faces. I'd forgotten how pongy it was.

"Well," says Andrea. She holds out her arms; I'm not sure whether she expects me to go to her or not. "My little Lollipop, all grown up!"

Lollipop. She called me Lollipop! Only Mum called me that. I look at her, uncertainly.

"This letter," she says. "I only wish I'd got it sooner! I'm afraid publishers are not always very good at sending things on."

I pick up a stripy cat and sit with him on my lap. I think he's Stripy Thomas, the one who causes all the trouble, stealing the other cats' food. He purrs, and kneads with his claws, making little pinpricks on my legs.

"I would have dropped everything and come immediately," says Andrea. "My poor Sue, she must have thought I didn't care!"

I know that I have to tell her. I swallow. "It was my fault," I whisper. I explain how Mum had given me the letter to post on my way to school. How I was in too much of a rush to do it on the way there, so I was planning to do it on my way back. "Only I didn't, cos… cos that was the day it happened."

"You mean…" Andrea hesitates.

"It was the day Mum died! I forgot all about the letter. I found it weeks later, in my school bag, and…

that's why you only just got it."

I hang my head, gazing down at Thomas's stripes. Grey, and white, and ginger. I wait for Andrea to say something. Is she going to be mad at me? I think I would be a bit mad at me. After all, Mum asked me specially. I knew it was important to her. I feel ashamed. I mumble that I'm sorry.

"No! Don't be." Andrea leans across and takes my hand. "I'm pleased that you've told me. I've been torturing myself, imagining your mum waiting for a telephone call, day after day, wondering why I never responded. I'm just so glad you posted the letter and didn't simply throw it away. Did your mum... did she show you what was in it?"

I say, "No – and I didn't read it!" I am anxious for her to know; I don't want Mum's friend thinking badly of me.

Andrea says soothingly that it's all right, she wouldn't have minded. "And I don't think your mum would, either. I have it here, you probably should read it, but I'll just tell you, very briefly, what it says. I gather your mum had been sick for some time?"

"Yes." I hold Stripy Tom's paws, to stop him kneading. "I was the one who looked after her!"

"I know." Andrea smiles. "She says in her letter… you're a daughter in a million. She couldn't have managed without you."

"And Stevie," I say.

"Yes, she mentions Stevie. She says no one could have asked for a better neighbour. But she was starting to get really worried in case… well! In case she became so poorly she had to go into care. Or if anything should happen to her. Who would be responsible for her little Lollipop? Obviously you couldn't stay with Stevie—"

"I could," I say. I stick a finger inside one of Tom's paws, wiggling it so that he splays his fingers. "I wouldn't have minded staying with Stevie!"

"Oh, Lol!" Andrea shakes her head. "They wouldn't have let you, sweetie. Even if Stevie had been willing, and… let's face it, she's not really a people person. And anyway, she's an old lady, it wouldn't have been fair. Your mum knew you couldn't stay with Stevie. What she was scared of was that you'd end up where you did, with your aunt and uncle. She loved her brother very much, but she really didn't think you'd be happy living there."

"I'm not!" I plonk Tom on the back of the chair, and suddenly it all comes bursting out of me in a great unstoppable flood. "I hate it," I cry. "I hate it, I HATE it!"

The tears are streaming down my cheeks. I'm sobbing and sobbing, an endless stream of tears. I fight to get back into my ice house, but it's no use, I can't find the way in. I give a desolate wail and collapse into Andrea's arms. She holds me, very close, stroking my hair and murmuring words of comfort. I'm crying too hard to hear what she says, but something is happening. A strange, half-remembered sensation is stealing over me. I feel loved, I feel safe!

"Oh, my poor little Lollipop!" Andrea takes out a

tissue and gently blots my eyes. "You've had a rough time of it. Let me tell you what your mum says in her letter. She says that if I'm agreeable – which I am! – she would like to appoint me as your guardian."

I stop crying, and start hiccupping. "You mean…" She hands me a tissue and I scrub, fiercely. "You mean I could… come and live with you?"

"That's what your mum dearly wanted. Unfortunately she didn't have time to make it official, but—"

"I'm not going back!" The tears come spurting out again. "I'm not ever going back! I'm not leaving Mr Pooter and I can't take him with me, and anyway I… I stole money out of Auntie Ellen's pot!"

"Oh, dear," says Andrea. She twitches her lips, like mock disapproving. "That sounds serious!"

I tell her that it was the only way I could get to Stevie's. "I had to rescue Mr Pooter!"

"Don't worry about the money," says Andrea. "I'll take care of that. The only problem as I see it is getting your Uncle Mark to agree to your living with me –

should you decide that you want to."

"I do want to!" The words come howling out of me.

"Yes, and I want you to," says Andrea. "Very much! But I think your uncle may point out that you don't really know me."

"I do!" I snatch my bag off the floor and scrabble round inside it until I find *Diary of a Nobody*. "Look!" I open it and show her. "*To Sue, with all my love, Andi. That's you, isn't it?*"

"Yes." She takes the book and stares at it with a kind of wonderment. "To think she kept it! All these years... This was almost the first present I ever gave her. It was one of my grandad's favourites, then it became one of mine."

"It was one of Mum's," I assure her. "We read it together loads of times. And something else!" I dip deep into a pile of T-shirts and pull out Blue Bunny. Rather shyly, cos I'm not absolutely certain, I say, "Were you the lady who gave me this?"

"I was." For a moment I think that she is going to cry

too. "It was the last time I ever saw you. Fancy you remembering!"

I feel I have to be honest, so I tell her that I only sort of remember.

"Well, of course," she says. "You were a tiny little thing. Oh, how I did miss you!" She hugs me to her. "You were going to be our very own little baby. Your mum's and mine. We were going to be a family. That was the plan."

I'm confused. "But what about my dad?"

Andrea says that my dad was quite happy. "He never really wanted to be a dad. Until you were actually born… and then he changed his mind. Couldn't resist you! So he and your mum got married, and – well! After a bit your dad decided he didn't want me seeing you any more. He said it upset your mum."

Indignantly I say, "*He* was the one that upset her!"

"Yes, sweetie, I know." Andrea takes my hand. "That's why I had to go away."

"Why?" The tears come welling back up. "I wish you hadn't!"

"Oh, Lol," she says, "I never wanted to. It nearly broke my heart, knowing I wasn't going to see you again. But it just made things so difficult for your mum. I didn't want to add to your problems. I loved your mum very very dearly."

I say, "More than my dad did!"

"That's probably true," agrees Andrea.

I glare at her, like it's somehow her fault. "Why did they ever get married?"

She shakes her head. "It seemed the right thing at the time."

I think to myself, *it didn't later*, but I don't say it in case it sets me off weeping again. I'm almost glad when Stevie punches the door open and in her usual aggressive tones says, "Still at it?"

"We're pretty well through," says Andrea.

Stevie grunts. "I suppose you'll be expecting a cup of tea." She stomps back down the hall. I give Andrea a watery grin.

"Her tea is *awful*. Mum used to say it tasted like

stale pond water."

"Well, we must just grit our teeth," says Andrea. "We don't want to hurt her feelings. Now, we must decide on a plan. I think what we shall have to do is leave Mr Pooter here for the time being—"

I stare at her, stricken. Leave Mr Pooter?

"Just until we can get things sorted. I promise you we'll come back for him as soon as we possibly can. We're not abandoning him. I wouldn't abandon Mr Pooter! Your mum and I had him when he was a tiny kitten. We'll come and fetch him, don't worry. In the meantime, he'll be quite safe with Stevie."

I know this is true; but I am still anxious. "Why can't we just take him with us?"

"To your aunt and uncle's?"

"No!" I thump, wildly, on the arm of the chair. "To your place!"

"The thing is, Lol." Andrea looks at me, gravely. "I can't just kidnap you, much as I should like to. We have to do everything strictly by the book. That means going back to speak with your uncle and seeing what we can arrange. It may even mean you have to stay there for another day or two—" she holds up a hand as I open my mouth to protest – "but I won't abandon you any more than I'll abandon Mr Pooter. I'll be there. If necessary, I'll book myself into a hotel. It's just that we have to do things properly if we want it all to work out. Fortunately your uncle knows me from the old days, so it's not like a total stranger turning up on the doorstep. And I have your mum's letter, so with any luck we'll be able to get things moving quite quickly – especially when he realises how you feel. It just means that you have to be brave for a little while longer. You have to trust me." She tips my face up towards her. "Do you trust me?"

I do. I feel, in an odd kind of way, that we've known each other for ever. That we're already friends. And besides, it's what Mum wanted.

"So let's just drink our pond water," says Andrea, "then leave poor old Stevie in peace."

CHAPTER TEN

It's the hardest thing I've ever had to do, coming back here with Andrea. We take a cab from the station, and as we get out I see that Uncle Mark's car is in the drive. My heart goes plummeting, right down to my shoes. They've come back early! I've been praying we would at least get here in time for me to tear up my note and for Andrea to put Auntie Ellen's money back. I start to tremble. Andrea stretches out her hand and takes hold of mine, and we go up the path together.

"Courage!" she whispers.

It's Auntie Ellen who opens the door. "So!" she snaps. "You decided to come back, did you?" She is very angry; I knew she would be. Partly she's angry cos of me taking her money, but also because she's been forced to come home early, all on my account.

"Dad was *worried* about you," says Holly.

It seems that after reading my note, Uncle Mark immediately rang Stevie to see if I was there. When we hear this, me and Andrea exchange glances. In spite of being scared, it's all I can do not to giggle. Stevie is always so *rude* on the phone.

"She gave me very short shrift," says Uncle Mark. "Practically boxed my ears… but at least I knew you were on your way back. Thank you for that," he adds, turning to Andrea. "It made me feel a bit better, knowing she was with you." He looks at me, reproachfully, like *how could you?* "You and I," he says, "are obviously going to have to have a bit of a chat."

Michael wants to know where Mr Pooter is. I tell him that he's with Stevie. "Just for the moment."

"Should have been left there in the first place," says Auntie Ellen. "It's what I've said all along."

My hand reaches out again for Andrea's. She gives it a reassuring squeeze. "Mark, I wonder," she says, "whether we could have that chat right now... just you and me. Could we do that?"

I clutch, rather desperately, at her arm. I don't want to be left alone with Auntie Ellen!

"Well, and maybe Laurel, too," says Andrea. "After all, she's the one it most concerns."

I don't think Auntie Ellen's very pleased at being excluded, but nobody invites her to join us so she gives one of her sniffs and takes her money pot out of the cupboard to check how much I've stolen.

"I'll pay you back!" I cry.

"I'll pay your aunt back," says Andrea. "Let's go, now,

and thrash things out. See if we can't come to some arrangement."

So that is what we do. Uncle Mark reads Mum's letter, nodding now and again and pursing his lips. I wait anxiously for his response.

"Right," he says. "Well!" Carefully, he folds the letter and gives it back to Andrea. "It's not such a bad idea, I suppose. It's true that Laurel's never really settled with us, and since it's what Sue wanted... I'd be quite agreeable, assuming you're both OK with it?"

"Oh, I think we are," says Andrea. "Aren't we?" She smiles at me, and I nod, vigorously.

"Well, in that case," says Uncle Mark, "let's give it a go. We'll see how it works out."

He's obviously relieved that he won't have to be responsible for me any more, though I don't have the feeling he actually wants to be rid of me. Just that he wants me to be happy, and he knows I never could be with him and Auntie Ellen.

He insists that we stay for a meal, which I don't really

want to and I'm not sure that Andrea does, either, but you have to be a little bit polite.

"Are you *going*?" says Holly.

Holly is not at all polite. Even Auntie Ellen tries to pretend that she's sad things didn't work out.

"It's just… you know… Laurel really didn't have what I would call a normal upbringing. But of course, you were Sue's friend, you knew what she was like. You'll be able to cope."

"I'm sure I shall," says Andrea.

As soon as we've eaten, we pack up a few more of my things and Uncle Mark takes us back to the station.

"Now, don't forget," he says, as he kisses me goodbye, "if things don't work out, you can always come back."

But I know, I just know, that they *will* work out. It's just this feeling I have.

I'm right. They do! I stay with Andi all through the summer, in her flat near the university where she teaches. We get Mr Pooter back from Stevie, and he's on his special diet, and he's taking his tablets, and he's not being sick any more, though even if he was, Andi wouldn't get mad at him. She loves Mr Pooter as much as I do. I'm never tired of hearing how she and Mum went to the local animal shelter to adopt a kitten, and how it was Mr Pooter who adopted *them*.

"He was such a tiny scrap, the smallest of the litter. But he stretched out his scrawny little arms and made these funny little squeaking noises, and we just knew that he was the one for us. We always meant to adopt another one, so he'd have a companion, but somehow we never got around to it, and then… well! It was all too late."

But it wasn't too late, cos now Mr Pooter has *two* catty companions. When we collected him from Stevie we found that a stray she had rescued had just had kittens, and she told us rather crossly that we had better take two of them.

"I don't want kittens getting under my feet! Not at my age."

So it was like we didn't really have much choice. As Andi says, you don't argue with Stevie. They are both black, which sometimes makes it quite difficult to tell them apart. "Is that Carrie?" we go. "Or is it Lupin?" I was the one who chose their names! They already answer to them.

We're all so happy together in Andi's flat, but the new school year is looming and I'm dreading what might be going to happen. Will I have to start all over again at yet another school? Or, worse still, will I have to go and live with Uncle Mark and Auntie Ellen again? I think to myself that I just couldn't bear it! But Andi has a surprise. She's rented a house near to Uncle Mark so that I can continue at the same school *and* we don't have to be separated. Hooray! It means that Andi has quite a long drive every day to get to work, but she says that she thinks it will be better if I don't have to cope with any more changes.

I am grateful for this as I am not good at changes, and I've sort of got used to Bennington. Also it means that I can still see Michael. He is a really nice boy. Some of the girls in my class tease me and say he's my boyfriend, but that is just totally not true. I am not into boys yet. Andrea says I will be, soon. Then, she says, there will be TROUBLE. I will be a regular, tiresome teenager!

I'm still a library assistant. I still have long talks about books with Mrs Caton, but I don't spend as much time in the library as I used to, mainly because I have now made some friends. Proper friends. Two new girls were put into our class, Janis and Elvi, and we have become quite close. Being new, they didn't realise that I was weird! Maybe I'm not, any more; at any rate, they don't seem to think so. I'm not called Dalek any more, either. Most people seem to call me Lol. That's OK! I don't mind.

Andi calls me Lollipop. Or sometimes Lolly. I feel as if I have known Andi all my life. We are hoping that next year she will be able to adopt me; then if I want I can be Laurel Stafford. I think I would rather have Andi's name than the name of my dad. I think it is what Mum would have liked. She would have been really pleased if she knew how things had turned out.

We now have all her books back. Michael got them down from the attic, and Uncle Mark and Auntie Ellen brought them over. Now that I am not living with her any more, Auntie Ellen doesn't seem to find me so irritating. She has become almost quite friendly. I will never be her sort of person; there is nothing much I can do about that. But when she kisses me hello or goodbye I no longer feel that she is gritting her teeth and just doing it as a duty. Last time she visited she said, "Well, things seem to be working out for you at last. I'm pleased about that. It really used to upset me, you were such a sad little ghost of a creature." So I think perhaps she is not so bad after all. Except for not liking cats!

Andi and me have put all Mum's books back in the open. They are free-range again! We are going out next week to buy a bookcase for them, as they are mostly on the floor at the moment. Andi has lots of books of her own, which I am exploring. She has also written one! It is rather learned; it is called *The Female Psyche in Time of War*. She was delighted to find that Mum had a copy of it. It was one of the ones that Michael brought down from the attic. I said that Mum used to keep it by the side of her bed, like it was something special.

"But it wasn't one we read together." To be honest, I can't really understand it. I've looked at it loads of times, but it is full of words I have never met before. Andi laughs and says, "Later!" And then she says, "Funny to think that I'd originally planned to write novels." I tell her that she should.

"You could write one about you and Mum! And me, when I was a baby."

I reckon that would make a really neat story. Andi has promised that she will think about it.

"Or if I don't do it," she says, "how about you?"

Hmm… I suppose I could.

I am sitting here now, on the sofa, with my laptop, wondering how to begin. Mr Pooter is curled up beside me. He is such a sweet old cat! When we got the kittens we were worried in case he felt that he was being pushed aside, but he is like a big daddy to them. They climb all over him, and just occasionally, when they are too rough or he has had enough, he smacks at them with his paw and they go skittering off.

One of them, Carrie, is sitting on top of my head. It is not very comfortable, as she keeps overbalancing and digging her claws in, which is actually quite painful, but I haven't the heart to move her. The other one, Lupin, is very interested in my laptop. He keeps dabbing with his paw and wer709yfoj62kouyh6#[1

That was Lupin, typing a row of nonsense. He is very interested in computers. Heq'#mhjnwp

That was him again! This obviously isn't going to work. Maybe I'll give up for now, and play with the kittens instead. It's not like there is any rush. But I *will* write the story. All about Andi and Sue who had a baby girl called Lollipop and a cat called Mr Pooter. I'll start it tomorrow…

STAR CRAZY ME!

I've wanted to be a pop star ever since I can remember –
well, a rock star actually, as I have a really BIG voice. My
nan used to say, *"That girl is star crazy!"*

I was sooo excited when I heard about the school talent contest.
I even wrote a special song with my friend Josh. But then the
meanest girl in the universe called me fat freak. I stormed out of
school and now I just want to go back...

978 000 715619 7

www.harpercollins.co.uk

FORTUNE COOKIE

It was Cookie that got us started on our life of crime.
Not that he was called Cookie back then. He was just the
puppy that lived next door. We didn't know that he would
soon be ours, and that we would have to save his life. Or
that he would lead us into such Big Trouble..."

A crazy adventure about friendship, family, pets – and a plan that
spirals out of control.

978 000 722462 3.

www.harpercollins.co.uk